D0867581

THE BRIDESMAID RESCUE

TEXAS HOTLINE SERIES, BOOK #3

JO GRAFFORD

GET A FREE BOOK!

Join my mailing list to be the first to know about new releases, free books, special discount prices, Bonus Content, and giveaways.

https://BookHip.com/JNNHTK

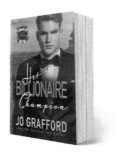

ACKNOWLEDGMENTS

Thank you to my incredible editor and friend, Cathleen Weaver. Another big thank you goes to my faithful beta reader and friend, Mahasani. Lastly, I want to give a shout-out to my Cuppa Jo Readers on Facebook for reading and loving my books!

ABOUT THIS SERIES

Welcome to the Texas Hotline, a team of search and rescue experts — police officers, firefighters, expert divers, and more. In an emergency, your sweet and swoon-worthy rescuer is only a phone call away.

CHAPTER 1: LOVE AT FIRST SIGHT

EMMA

Late June

I'm in serious trouble. At least Emma Taylor's heart was. It was speeding like a sprint car around a racetrack at the way the tall, dark Marine was gazing at her. *What is wrong with me?* Maybe she was tired, or maybe she hadn't chugged enough coffee this morning, because an encounter with a fellow soldier never had this effect on her. Not once in her eight years of service to the U.S. Marines, at any rate.

As a military police officer deployed to Afghanistan, she was accustomed to dealing with hundreds of soldiers every day. Sometimes thousands. So what was so special about this one? She didn't even know the guy's name. Not that she couldn't take a quick peek at his name tag after she and her police dog, Scout, finished circling his Humvee.

Beneath her lashes, she noted that the Marine was standing back the appropriate dozen feet or so, giving her and her K9 partner the space they required to inspect his vehicle in the crowded middle lane of the checkpoint. He wasn't hovering over her in that annoying way some soldiers did, as if standing closer to a police officer somehow provided them with an extra measure of security in this God-forsaken corner of the world.

The truth was, she was just as exposed to a stray missile as anyone else. The nine millimeter caliber pistol strapped inside her holster didn't have the faintest hope of protecting her from the blast of a bomb or a grenade. Nope. Her safety rested squarely in the hands of the very soldiers whose long lines of vehicles she was currently processing.

Their fire power and bravery was all that stood between the checkpoint she helped run and the enemy lines they would be heading toward next. Her MP station would serve as their last stop before they headed south to Kandahar — into the heart of enemy territory.

As Emma worked, she tried not to think about the dangers that the handsome Marine and his comrades would soon be facing. She'd learned a long time ago to just do her job. Her personal rules for maintaining her sanity during war were simple:

Don't memorize names. Don't try to remember faces. Don't get too attached. Most of these guys (along with the handful of gals in their ranks) she would never see again.

That was a good thing, because she wouldn't ever have to know which ones made it home in one piece and which ones would be returned in a box. Well, normally it was a good thing not to know stuff like that, but she suddenly found herself breaking one of her personal rules and wishing like crazy that one Marine in particular would, in fact, make it home safely.

"Any chance you can shed some light on what you and your dog are looking for, Officer Taylor?"

Emma blinked as the tall Black man in question strode across the lane in her direction. Gosh, but he was swoony! All broad and ripped beneath his sand-colored camouflage uniform. The morning rays beat down on his sun-kissed features, accentuating the angle of his jaw and his squared-off chin. The brim of his hat was pulled just low enough over his eyes that it was hard to read his expression. He sounded Texan, but she was guessing he also had some island blood in him.

"Who says we're looking for anything, Sergeant..." Emma allowed her gaze to drop to his name tape. "Zane." *Wow!* A name with a Z. His last name was as gorgeous as the rest of him.

Her heartbeat sped at his nearness. There was just so much of him, though it wasn't merely his size affecting her senses. It was something more — a special brand of awareness zinging between them. She wondered again what was wrong with her this morning. *No emotional strings. Just do your job, Emma. You're not his wife, fiancée, or girlfriend.* But there was a part of her that wished she was. Or at least something more to him than a random MP at a random checkpoint.

"I do, ma'am." He was close enough for her to see his eyes now. His dark, coffee-brew gaze swept her face and instantly registered male admiration. "You've circled my vehicle three times already."

"Did I?" she pretended innocence, trying to sound offhand. "Guess I like to be thorough, sergeant."

"Marcus," he corrected without missing a beat. "Marcus Zane. So did I pass the test, or are you about to whip out your cuffs?" His lips twisted into a half-smile, and his baritone drawl held a note of humor. However, there was a no-nonsense look in his eyes that told her he very much understood the dangers he would soon be facing.

She chuckled, liking how smoothly he'd slipped his first name into the conversation. It wasn't necessary for her to know it, but she was every shade of thrilled to realize that he wanted her to. "Aw, are you flirting with me, sergeant?" She lowered her voice so that none of the other soldiers milling around could hear her words.

"We're at war, ma'am," he shot back, pressing a hand to his chest in mock indignation. "Sorry, but there's no time to flirt with a beautiful woman."

You think I'm beautiful, huh? She felt a wave of warmth travel across her cheeks that had nothing to do with the desert heat radiating off the sand surrounding them. "Thank you." She let out the breath she'd been holding. "You wouldn't believe the offers I get sometimes." Or the desperate pleadings from a few very young, very cocky, very scared soldiers right before they crossed into enemy territory. She'd been proposed to at least a dozen times this week already, by men desperate to have a reason for Divine Providence to keep them alive in the coming days.

"Oh, I probably would." He snorted. "I've spent enough years working around dudes. Not to mention, I happen to be one, myself."

"I noticed," she returned dryly.

"Good. Mission accomplished." Ignoring Scout's warning growl, he fell into step beside her.

Though Emma had already mentally cleared both Sergeant Zane and his vehicle for moving on, she couldn't see any harm in detaining him a few minutes longer by making a fourth pass around his Humvee. His unit wasn't scheduled to depart for another hour, and neither of them was in a hurry to end their flirt session. That's what it was. There was no point in lying to herself.

He dipped his dark head closer to hers, ignoring another growl from Scout. "Since you dodged my first question, I don't suppose the extra attention you're giving me and my men has anything to do with the very important package we're transporting?"

She glanced up in surprise, no longer pretending to inspect his vehicle. "You know about the package?" The prisoner his unit was escorting was in the central Humvee, three vehicles back from his. His situation was highly classified, so she doubted many soldiers in his unit had received the full briefing on the man's identity or the reason he was being transported.

Marcus Zane's dark brows shot up. He gave a low whistle. "I do now, Officer Taylor. I had my suspicions before, but..."

"Emma," she interrupted, hoping to distract him from his bulldog pursuit of details about their prisoner. "And you can quit pretending that I just made a major slip-up, in the hopes of wheedling more information out of me. It's one of those need-to-know things. I don't make the rules." Her gut told her that he not only needed to know, but that he already knew. His adept way at maneuvering their conversation was more about establishing common ground between them, and quickly, since he had less than an hour to spare. Kind of genius, actually. And wildly flattering.

"Emma," he repeated softly. His dark gaze roved over her face again. "I'm really glad you decided your name was on my list of need-to-know items. I like it, by the way. It suits you."

He didn't offer any of the cheesy compliments she was accustomed to receiving. Just a simple *I like it.* Her insides melted a few more degrees at the genuine note in his voice. "Nice to know," she teased, "since I'm sorta stuck with it."

"So..." He canted his broad frame in her direction, eliciting a third, damp-sounding snarl from Scout.

She tugged the agitated German Shepherd back a few inches and gave him the signal to heel.

"Now, who's flirting?" Marcus teased, eyeing her movements. "You just ordered your dog not to devour me, didn't you?"

"Something like that." She smiled sadly as she glanced around them, taking in the serious expressions on the faces of his comrades. "Unfortunately, this isn't a breakfast date, and I don't see a napkin to scrawl my phone number on." He was shipping out in a matter of minutes.

"That's alright. I have a very good memory and no plans to forget you." His gaze caressed hers. It felt as intimate as if their hands had touched.

"What are you doing?" she whispered, hating the

fact that she was blushing and hoping no one was watching them too closely.

"With your permission, I'd like to kiss you inside my head before I go."

Her lips parted on a breathy chuckle. "Most guys don't ask for permission before imagining themselves doing far more than that." Not all that surprising, considering how few females there were around.

"Yeah, well, I happen to have higher standards than that," he returned in his lazy drawl. "Much higher. In fact, I'm only going to kiss you if you agree to kiss me back."

What? She gave another breathless laugh but didn't drop her gaze from his. They shared a highly charged, heart-racing moment.

"And only after you recite your phone number, so I can memorize it."

She shook her head at him, her smile widening. He had to know her cell phone wouldn't work on this side of the world. It wasn't going to work until she returned stateside, which could be months from now.

In a soft voice hitched with emotion, she quickly rattled off her number.

He bent his head over hers, canting it slightly as if he was swooping in for a kiss, but he stopped several inches away. "This is the part where you kiss me back, Emma Taylor."

He never touched her. He didn't close his eyes, either, but she felt thoroughly kissed after he raised his head. "So am I the first Black guy you've ever necked with?"

She gasped at the brazen question. "Does it matter?" No, she'd never dated a Black guy before. Then again, she hadn't done much dating since high school. Between boot camp, MP training, dog handler school, and deployments, there hadn't been time for exploring many personal relationships. Or maybe she just hadn't met the right guy. Until now.

"To me it does. I want to be your first."

"Marcus," she whispered in an agonized voice, knowing she'd let things go far enough between them. She'd already broken every single one of her personal rules about getting too close to a fellow soldier.

"And your last," he added swiftly, dipping his head to gaze deeply into her eyes. "In case you're wondering, I'm gunning for the spot as the *only* guy in your life."

A shaky sound of mirth escaped her. "Poor Dad." *Don't do this, Marcus.* What he was about to face in battle would be hard enough. He didn't need her as a distraction inside his head.

Marcus snickered. "Maybe he and I can work something out." He made a face. "I get ninety-nine percent of your attention. He gets a solid one percent."

"You're going to have to do better than that," she confessed shyly. "I'm an only child, so he's very territorial." And that was putting it mildly. Dad had always been her biggest and loudest cheerleader, her unwavering supporter of everything she tried — though he was no more thrilled about her decision to join the military than her lifelong circle of friends had been.

"Fine! Two percent to my ninety-eight. You drive a hard bargain, woman." His teasing baritone resonated deliciously through her.

Though she smiled again, her thoughts were already leaping ahead to reality. "I wish you the best, Marcus. I truly do. With whatever lovely gal you end up with." She knew they weren't likely to see each other again.

"Thank you," he retorted cheerfully. "Is that a challenge, beautiful?"

"No, it's..." She sighed. *Goodbye*.

"I'm going to call you, Emma." He expression grew serious as he mimed the act of lifting a phone to his ear. "Your number is permanently seared into my memory. Promise. I just can't tell you exactly when."

And now he was making promises he probably wouldn't be able to keep.

"It's been really nice meeting you, Marcus." For some reason, she couldn't bring herself to tell him goodbye. It sounded too foreboding, considering their current circumstances. Too final.

His upper lip curled. "I can do better than nice.

Just wait until I follow up that kiss inside my head with the hands-on version."

Okay, now I'm swooning on the inside. "A real one next time, huh?" she teased. Did he seriously envision a next time between them? It was preposterous and slightly insane to consider their brief encounter the start of something, but golly! He wasn't kidding. It sure felt like something, virtual kiss and all.

"I'd prefer to call it our second kiss. I think we both know the first one already happened."

She pursed her lips and pretended to consider his words. "On a scale of one to ten in the romance department, it wasn't too shabby."

"Oh, now you're judging me?" His dark gaze turned wicked.

"That's what you wanted, you cocky Texan." She playfully waggled a finger at him. "Don't bother trying to deny it. You wanted my attention, Marcus Zane, and you got it."

He looked so self-satisfied that she laughed again. "I hope that means you believe I'm going to call you?"

She made a face and glanced away. "I've never been a wait-beside-the-phone kinda gal. I'm more of grab-life-by-the-horns kinda one."

His voice dropped to a lower, huskier tenor. "Our next kiss will be the kind that's worth waiting for. Trust me."

Her mouth went dry as her head spun back to his. "What makes you so sure?"

"I just know, Emma. One look at you. That's all it took."

The way he was looking at her now was doing ridiculous things to her heart. Things neither of them had any business feeling on a sandy road facing Kandahar.

She gave him a measuring look, foolishly wanting to believe the fairytale promise he was trying to hand her. "How about we make a deal? You call me, and I'll believe you then. No more doubts. No more questions."

"I will." He started to give her a two-fingered salute, but a male whoop of joy made him pause.

CHAPTER 2: THE SACRIFICE

EMMA

"Emma? Emma Taylor?"

She spun around at the familiar voice. "Omigosh! Hunt?" Her heart leaped with excitement to see a face she recognized. Hunt Ryker had been a fellow student in her dog handler course several years ago. They'd studied together for tests and had partnered up for one of the hardest urban warfare challenges at the end. To this day, she credited him for helping her pass the rigorous certification requirements. Unfortunately, they'd lost touch after they graduated. Military duty and frequent moves had a way of doing that to friends in uniform.

His tall, rangy form barreled in her direction. Bypassing Marcus, he reached out to enclose her in a bear hug, knocking the brim of his hat sideways.

She hugged him back, then laughingly reached up to straighten his cap. "So the Marines haven't run you out yet?" From time-to-time, he'd crossed her mind, and she'd wondered if he was still serving.

His burnished Apache features laughed back. "Living the dream, baby! Long hours. Low pay. What's there not to love about it?"

Marcus's fist came out to tap him playfully on the shoulder. "Hey, don't forget about all the free round-trip tickets to sandy, exotic locales." He winked at Emma, making her catch her breath all over again at how handsome he was when he smiled.

"If by exotic, you mean getting sand in all the places God never intended..." Another hunky Marine shouldered his way into their circle, claiming their attention. When his hazel gaze landed on Emma, he gave a low, admiring whistle. "Okay. Maybe this place isn't the deepest armpit of the world, after all." He shoved one large paw in her direction. "I'm Axel Hammerstone, by the way."

As she shook his hand, her gaze flickered back to Marcus. "Nice to meet you, Axel." There was an easy camaraderie among these soldiers that told her they were more than battle buddies. They were Marcus's friends. Close ones.

A fourth soldier jogged in their direction. "Hey! Did I miss my invitation to the party, or what?" His auburn hair caught the morning sun and flashed like fire for a moment.

Hunt faked a boxing stance at the man's approach. "This is Digby MacLamore, or Dig as everyone likes to call him for reasons I don't have time to go into. Short version is he had the audacity to make my sister fall in love with him, thereby obligating me to cover his sorry hide with my M60 in the coming days."

Dig rolled his eyes. "I'm also the lucky guy who gets to drive these jokers across the desert. They better hope I don't hit too many ruts." He was wearing a wedding ring, which meant he'd done more than fall in love. He'd gone and married Hunt's sister.

For a moment, Emma's heart constricted with envy over the bond these men shared as they headed into battle. Her gut told her they would have each other's backs every second of every day, which for some reason reminded her of how desperately alone she was in the world.

There was only one other woman currently deployed with her MP unit, and they'd never gotten along very well. Missy Cole, a petite spitfire of a medic, was all too content with being surrounded by mostly men. In fact, Emma sometimes got the impression Missy would've preferred to be the only female around. So in addition to not having a boyfriend, fiancé or husband, Emma also did not have a true battle buddy.

Hunt scuffled a moment with his brother-in-law, then turned back to her. "Besides being tickled to death about seeing you again, the reason I headed over here was to ensure this player wasn't giving you too much trouble." He waggled his brows in Marcus's direction.

"A player, huh?" She made a face at Marcus. "I believe you left that part out during your introduction."

The smoldering look he sent her way made her curl her toes in her boots. "Let's just say I'm a grab-life-by-the-horns kinda guy."

She chuckled at the way he so cleverly slung her own words from earlier back at her. "Yeah, I'm starting to see that. Got yourself a reputation to go with it and everything."

He made a scoffing sound. "Didn't see a ring on your finger, beautiful." He glanced down at her hand and back up again. "Nope. Still don't see one."

"So you *did* cut the fool with her." Hunt snorted and shook his head at Marcus. "Good thing you have friends, bro, in case we have to fend off a rabid boyfriend, at some point."

"Boyfriend!" Marcus folded his arms and shot her a half-teasing, half-challenging look. "You didn't say anything about a boyfriend!"

She grinned back. "You didn't ask."

"Burn!" Axel gave another one of his low whistles.

Marcus's smile slipped a degree as he met and held Emma's gaze. "So is there?"

"Is there what?" she taunted softly.

"Any competition I need to worry about?"

She held his gorgeous dark gaze a moment longer. "There might be someone special," she finally admitted, allowing her eyes to finish what she left unsaid.

"So, ah, I hate to break up whatever this is, but..." Hunt stepped between them, eyes twinkling, and angled his head toward their Humvee. "Gotta war to fight."

She nodded, sobering. "Be safe out there, you guys."

Hunt nodded and fist-bumped her. "You betcha. We promise to keep 'em so occupied on the front lines that your crew shouldn't have much to worry about back here."

She turned to Marcus as his friends jogged to their vehicle. "Any chance you'll promise me no stupid heroics?"

He cocked his head at her. "You know I can't, beautiful. The only promise I can make is to call you when it's over."

She blinked, feeling her eyes mist. "You better not leave me waiting too long by the phone."

He caressed her with his eyes one last time. "Yours will be the first number I dial."

A honk sounded.

"I promise," he finished quietly. Then he spun on his boots and strode to the waiting vehicle.

She watched as he rejoined his friends and

hopped aboard. He waved as his unit revved their engines and rolled away from her checkpoint.

"See something you like there, Taylor?"

Emma stiffened at her company commander's words. She hadn't heard Captain Miller's approach. He was a really nice guy, someone she respected enormously, but she wasn't in the mood to joke around about what had just happened between her and Sergeant Marcus Zane.

"Does it ever get any easier, sir?" she muttered.

"What? Dating a soldier?"

"I'm not dating anyone, sir. You know that." Her scowl was for his benefit, though she still couldn't bring herself to tear her gaze away from the swiftly departing Marine unit. "I was referring to how hard it is to watch young, hopeful soldiers head into battle." She batted the air with her hand. "It's nothing like those video games they played while growing up. They'll be taking real bullets this time. No re-spawning and hopping right back to their feet."

"Yeah, I hear you, sergeant. And, no. It doesn't get any easier." The hoarseness in his voice made her gaze flit briefly in his direction.

"What's going on, sir?" Her gut told her they were no longer talking about the Marines who were busy disappearing into a cloud of dust and sand on the horizon.

He angled his head in the direction of the guard

shack. "Follow me, sergeant. You're at least two hours overdue for a break."

"It's okay, sir. I know we're not working the cash registers at Walmart. This is war."

"Yeah, well, you'll still remain hydrated and in your best fighting form under my watch, soldier. So if I say you're on break, you're on break."

"Roger that, sir." Scout gave a yip of excitement, indicating he was happy to finally be moving again. He trotted obediently at Emma's side, knowing from past experience that there would be refreshments for him on the other side of the tent walls of their head-quarters.

Captain Miller lowered his head as they trudged side-by-side through the sand. "This isn't something I wanted to broadcast out there to the rest of the unit, but it's my fiancée. She emailed me earlier to let me know she received her deployment orders."

Welcome to the club! Emma grimaced. It seemed as if everyone in uniform was getting deployed these days. "Aw, that's tough, sir. Sorry to hear it." His fiancée was an Army nurse stationed at Ft. Hood, Texas. The war had been pretty difficult on their relationship. Like two ships passing in the wind, they couldn't seem to catch a break on their military orders. It seemed as if they were always just missing each other.

"Yeah. I was sorry to hear it, too. She's excited, though. Says it's what she always trained for. I guess

I'm torn. Happy that she's getting what she wants, but..." He paused to hold aside the canvas tent flap for Emma.

She nodded, understanding what he left unsaid, and stepped past him. She led Scout across the main gathering room of what they all referred to as the guard shack, though it was technically nothing more than a large, sand-colored tent.

She knew the captain was sad that he and his fiancée couldn't be together more often. "Guess we better hurry up and win this war, so we can all get back to our normal lives." She wasn't sure her words would provide any comfort, but that was the best she could offer her boss at the moment.

He gave a long-suffering huff as he tossed his cap into a chair and headed for the coffee machine. They were in the main gathering room they used for meal times and group meetings. His private office was in the back part of the tent, an area that had been partitioned off.

She removed Scout's leash and harness, refilled his water bowl, and doled out a few of his favorite snacks.

"In some ways, I envy the fact that you're still single and unattached. Life was simpler for me back in those days." Captain Miller poured two cups of coffee and handed her one.

"And lonelier," she reminded, tipping up her cup for a sip. It was hot, but it was caffeinated. She could use the pick-me-up after being emotionally peeled back one layer at a time by Sergeant Zane during the past hour.

"But peaceful. Once you fall in love, you have something to lose."

Yeah. Thanks to meeting Marcus today, she was starting to get some idea of what it meant to have someone in the war to lose. Normally, she would have teasingly ragged her captain about rubbing her nose in the fact he was happily engaged, but not today. Her throat was too constricted with worry about the dangers Marcus and his friends were heading into.

There'd been rumbling on the MP radios all morning about movement in the mountains. Many times those rumblings turned out to be nothing more than small clusters of nomads making their way to and from Kandahar. But what if today's movement indicated something more ominous? The war had scattered a significant number of terrorists throughout the mountains, too, and they had a horrible habit of popping up at the most importune times. The number of suicide bombings and attacks on Western peacekeeping forces had been on the rise for months.

"You're awfully quiet, all of a sudden." Her commander treated her to an amused, sideways glance as he took a seat at the folding table in the center of the room. "Normally, you're Miss Sunshine and Chatter. I'm starting to think a certain tall, dark Marine might've gotten to you a little more than you're willing to admit."

She blew out a breath and joined him at the table. "He said he wanted to call me," she confessed as she slid into her seat, "and I was crazy enough to give him my number." She hunched over her cup of coffee, waiting for the fireworks.

"Whoa!" Her commander set down his coffee mug with a thud. She had his full attention now. "Let me get this straight." His brown eyebrows shot straight up. "You gave out your number? You? To a single, datable guy?"

"That's what I said, sir," she returned sheepishly, not quite meeting his gaze.

He shook his head in disbelief, sitting back in his chair to study her with interest. "What is the world coming to?" He was shorter than average, but he more than made up for it in toughness. A former boxer, he'd gotten their MP unit prepared for their current deployment the old-fashioned way — through blood, sweat, and tears. Her body still ached every time she thought about the punishing hours of weight lifting he'd put them through at the gym, along with the endless miles of running. And don't get her started on their nonstop excursions to various obstacle courses, the firing range, and the field.

After an uncomfortable silence, Emma muttered,

"May we please forget we ever had this conversation, sir?"

He smirked. "I can, but you won't."

True. She hated the fact that he was right, and she also hated the fact that he knew he was right.

"So what's your story, Sergeant Taylor?"

"My story, sir?" She quirked a brow at him.

"Yeah. You got someone waiting for you back home, or what?"

Her eyes widened at the fact that her commander was actually nosing around her private life. It was unlike him. Sure, they talked about work and sports, and he had a terrible habit of going on and on about the love of his life sometimes. However, he'd never once poked around in her personal business during the entire two years they'd worked together.

"Sorry for prying, but you're my responsibility and I'll admit to worrying about you sometimes."

"Worrying, sir!" She was aghast. *Holy smokes!* She did her job and did it well. As far as she could tell, she'd never given him a moment to doubt her commitment to the Marines.

"Just doing my job, sergeant." He held up his hands in mock defense. "I know things haven't been easy for you since your mom passed. Still, I'll admit to being a little surprised when you arrived alone at the airfield on our way here." He eyed her in concern. "You had a pretty massive showing of friends at your promotion ceremony not too long ago, then boom. Not a single person at your deployment send-off. What's up with that?"

She took another sip of her coffee. "Dad hosted a shindig for me and my friends the night before. I'm not a big fan of tearful goodbyes." Especially not the public kind. It was beyond her comprehension why so many military families put each other through the emotional wringer of making posters and inviting every sibling, grandparent, and cousin to those sorts of things.

"Me, neither, but most folks still have a significant other show up for the final countdown." His own fiancée had been in attendance at their send-off.

She shook her head and peered down into her coffee mug. "I made Dad stay home. Figured he'd been through enough, sir." They'd only buried Mom a little over a year ago.

"Meaning there's no special someone in your life, outside of your family, eh?"

Emma gave her commander a tight smile over the rim of her mug. "We'll see...if he calls."

He looked intrigued. "I take it, we're talking about Mr. Tall, Dark, and Charming again?"

"Maybe." She took a noisy sip, hoping he'd change the subject.

The tent flap to the guard shack was abruptly yanked open. "Captain?" A young corporal appeared, pushing back his hat with a worried look.

"I think you should come take a look outside. There's been an explosion."

"What sort of explosion?" Captain Miller shot out of his chair.

Emma followed them past the tent flap.

"I dunno, sir. It's a couple of miles out, I'd say." The corporal led them outside and pointed in the direction that the last Marine convoy had traveled.

Emma's stomach felt sick at the puffs of black smoke rising in the distance. The wind was whipping in their direction, carrying the scent of something burning.

Captain Miller whipped out his radio and called for an inquiry into the status of the Marines heading toward Kandahar.

For a moment, all Emma could hear was static on the other end. Then there were a few frantic shouts.

She managed to make out the words *ambush* and *under attack*.

For the next several minutes, it was every hand on deck at the MP station, as Emma and her fellow police officers attempted to help coordinate an emergency evacuation. Helicopters rumbled overhead, and a trio of bomber jets did a few fly-by passes.

She mechanically went through the motions, though her heart was numb. *Don't get attached.* If only she'd stuck to her own rules and not allowed Marcus Zane to get close enough to matter to her.

But she had, and now her heart was bleeding with worry.

A headache pounded between her temples as the morning wore into the afternoon. A detail of MPs was eventually sent to the scene with a pack of search and rescue dogs. For some reason, Captain Miller didn't choose Emma to go along.

"Sergeant Taylor, I need to see you in the guard shack." Though his voice was deathly calm, it sliced through her as if he'd been shouting at the top of his lungs. She knew that tone, and it portended nothing good.

"Yes, sir." She nodded at Missy Cole, who was gearing up to head to the scene of the explosion.

"Don't worry, sir. We got this." Missy smirked and glanced knowingly between Emma and Captain Miller. In her relentless and infuriating way, she'd been trying for days to get Emma to admit there was something going on between her and their company commander. Something romantic and inappropriate, which couldn't have been further from the truth.

Blocking out the woman's spiteful expression, Emma headed for the shack, her heart pounding with dread.

"Why are you making me sit this one out, sir?" She spoke through stiff lips, fearing the worst.

"I think you know why." He led her back to his private office. "Sit."

"How bad is it?" Her voice shook at she took a seat and clasped her hands tightly in her lap.

"I have a list of causalities, Taylor, so if you have any names you want to run past me..." He gestured helplessly.

Right. He needed to know the identities of the soldiers she'd been visiting with to confirm whether they were on his list.

For some reason, Emma was unable to start with Marcus. "I, ah...went to dog handler school with Sergeant Hunt Ryker."

Captain Miller nodded, looking grave. "He's injured. Mostly burns from the explosion. They air lifted him out a while ago."

Tears of anguish burned behind her eyelids. It seemed like only minutes ago they'd been laughing and talking next to his Humvee.

She drew a jagged breath and continued, "He introduced me to his brother-in-law. A driver by the name of Digby MacLamore." She could still picture the cheery twinkle in the Irish man's eyes.

Captain Miller shook his head. "I'm sorry, but that one's listed as missing in action."

"Missing," she repeated carefully. "Can you be more specific?"

He shrugged. "It was an explosion. You and I both know it'll take a while for us to process the scene."

Meaning he doubted the man was still alive. She

pressed a hand to her chest and nodded. It was getting harder to breathe. "There was another friend they introduced me to. Axel Hammer-something or another."

He scrolled the screen of his iPad. "Hammerstone."

"That sounds right, sir."

"Shot up pretty bad. He's been air lifted out, too."

The dread in Emma's chest thickened to a full broil. If Marcus's dearest friends were all critically injured or missing, she knew it didn't bode well for his survival.

Captain Miller drummed his fingers against his iPad. "As for Sergeant Marcus Zane..." His face was pale.

"I don't think I can hear this, sir," she whispered, half-rising from her chair.

"His current status is missing in action, but..."

But what? She dropped limply back into her seat, bracing for the worst.

"They're not expecting him to remain missing for long. He and another soldier were knocked over the edge of a cliff during the explosion. Not clear on the details yet, but there's a rumor flying around that he sacrificed himself to save the other guy. I'm sorry, but they don't anticipate finding him alive, my friend."

She closed her eyes, making no attempt to swipe

at the hot tears coursing down her cheeks. *No stupid heroics.* She'd tried to get Marcus to promise her, but he'd refused.

"Looks like you gave your phone number to a real American hero, Sergeant Taylor."

She drew a shuddering breath and started to weep silently. Part of her was glad she'd made the ridiculously brave Marine happy right before he'd paid the ultimate price. The other part of her was shattered.

It meant he wouldn't be able to keep his promise. There wouldn't be any phone calls from him. *Ever.* Not even if she sat by the phone until she was old and gray.

CHAPTER 3: BRIDESMAID AGAIN

EMMA

Late September

Emma stood in front of the long mirror Clara Hudson's fiancé had dragged from the master bedroom to the great room inside the beach house where she and her friends were gathered. The wedding would start at the water's edge in less than an hour. The sun would be setting by then.

She entwined her fingers in the champagne-colored silk length of her bridesmaid dress. It was an off-the-shoulder ensemble that boasted a gauzy bodice overlay. She was surprised at how attractive and form-fitting it was, how perfectly it set off her late summer tan. In some of the past weddings she'd been a part of, she could've sworn the bride had outfitted her in the most atrocious bridesmaid dress possible to ensure she wouldn't outshine the bride.

"You look amazing, Em." Clara glided across the room to stand beside her in front of the mirror. She wasn't the kind of woman who worried about stuff like that. A modern-day hippie, she'd always been perfectly comfortable in her own skin. She looked like a fairytale creature this evening, with white rose-buds and fragile green vines threaded through her waist-length hair.

"It's sweet of you to say that." Emma slid her arm around her best friend's slender waist and leaned in to lightly press their cheeks together — pink silk next to white silk, velvet brown eyes next to pools of sea-blue. Both were sun-bleached blondes, but hers was only shoulder-length, a more practical style for military life. "Even though we both know it's not true."

Clara blinked. Genuine surprise radiated across her fine-boned features. "Please tell me you're kidding."

Emma sighed. "I wish, but no amount of makeup can hide this." She waved at the blue and black smudges beneath her eyes. She hadn't slept well since her deployment to Afghanistan. There was nothing quite like going to bed each night with a cell phone clutched to one's chest, waiting for a ghost to call. Her gaze dipped to her too-thin frame. "Or how much weight I've lost, since I purchased this dress."

"I know." Sadness infused Clara's voice. "It doesn't make you any less beautiful, though." She lifted a hand to wag a finger at her friend's reflection.

"Shake that pretty head all you want, but it won't change the fact that today I had no less than three of my single guy friends ask me — correction, *beg* me — to hook them up with my hottie hot Marine friend."

Emma rolled her eyes. "Now you're just messing with me."

"My stepbrother was one of them."

Emma's lips parted in surprise. "You mean Lincoln?"

"No, the prince of Arabia." Clara straightened to scowl at her reflection. "Of course I mean Lincoln. He's the only stepbrother I have." She pursed her hot pink lacquered lips. "He wants to date you, Em."

"I..." Emma shifted uncomfortably from one bare foot to the other. Lincoln was a really great guy, a cop like her but on the civilian side of things. "I can't." Her lack of footwear was one of Clara's hippie requirements for this evening's attire. The wedding party would be standing barefoot in the sand during the coming ceremony.

"Yes, you can, darling," her friend pressed. The concern in her gaze deepened.

"I mean, I choose not to." Clara, of all people, knew her reasons. Or at least her biggest reason — Marcus Zane.

"Then make another choice."

Emma's teeth sank into her lower lip to keep it from trembling. She lowered her voice, trying a different tactic. "Today's not about me. It's about you." Why couldn't Clara just let things go and focus on getting married?

"Exactly. And there's nothing that would make this bride happier than to see my maid of honor happy. Not to mention, I totally owe you for introducing me to Owen." Owen Banks was the Marine she'd be marrying in approximately forty-five minutes. A Marine who had known and served with Marcus. He was one of the few soldiers who hadn't been injured during the ambush.

"Well, dating someone else isn't going to make me happy." Emma made a face at her friend. "I'm sorry, but I'm not ready. It's too soon."

"You never even dated Marcus. You said so, yourself," Clara protested. "You only met him once."

"I guess it was one of those love-at-first-sight things, then," Emma sighed. *Just let it go already. Please?*

Her friend looked pained. "He's gone, Em."

"No. He's MIA. There's a difference."

Clara gave a sad, half-shake of her head. "He fell off a cliff, sweetie."

He'd voluntarily let go to save a friend's life. Again, there was a difference. "They never recovered his body," she reminded stiffly, closing her eyes to block out the pity in her friend's gaze.

"Oh, Em! Why do you insist on torturing yourself like this?" Clara's voice grew suspicious, making Emma's eyelids snap open. "Have you even bothered going to those grief counseling sessions I set up for you?"

"Yes, but only because I love you. Not because I see any point in going." *Because I'm not grieving.* She lowered her arm from Clara's waist and took a step back, indicating that their conversation was coming to a close.

Clara huffed out a breath. "You can't sit beside the phone forever."

"I won't. Promise." *I'm only doing it until he calls.*

A wary smile tugged at the lips of the bride-to-be. "Well, as you pointed out, I gotta focus on getting married right now."

"Hear, hear!" An impatient female voice chimed in from behind them. It was her younger sister, Tinsley.

"But we're not done with this conversation, Em." Clara shook her finger in warning again before spinning around to allow Tinsley, a professional makeup artist, to re-powder her nose and touch up her mascara.

AS THE BRIDE had so meticulously planned, the sun was just starting to set when the wedding party gathered at the water's edge. It was a truly gorgeous scene. The harshest rays of the sun had been reduced to muted orange and purple streaks across the sky, turning the strand to glistening gold. And there was something entirely magical about the feel of warm sand between their toes.

Though Emma was exhausted from so many weeks without a decent night's sleep, the lap of ocean waves against the beach brought a sense of peace she hadn't felt in a long time. God's own therapy. *Hmm.* Maybe she should have ditched all those counseling sessions and headed for the beach eons ago. With the sense of peace, however, came an unexpected wave of sleepiness that made her sway on her feet.

Lincoln Hudson's hand tightened on her elbow. He was standing beside her, since he was serving as Clara and Owen's best man. He bent to whisper in her ear. "You doing okay there?"

She blinked a few times to ward off the webs of sleep. Forcing a smile, she glanced up at him to nod.

The concern-infused admiration in his expression made her quickly drop her gaze. Apparently, Clara hadn't been stretching the truth about Lincoln's interest in her. It was way too bad. She swallowed a sigh. Under normal circumstances, she wouldn't have hesitated to go to dinner or the movies with such a nice guy. He wasn't hard on the eyes, either — all blonde and chiseled beneath the unpadded shoulders of his tuxedo jacket.

But these weren't normal circumstances, and...

Emma blinked again, this time not because she was tired. There was something glinting in the distance, something that brought out every soldierly instinct in her. Maybe she was more tired than she realized. Heck, maybe she was hallucinating, because she could have sworn it was the glint of a sniper rifle from the top of the resort building ahead. Moments later, a second glint appeared from an elevated sand dune across from it. Behind the glint was the long, shadowy figure of a...what? Logic told her it had to be a piece of driftwood, though it sure resembled a man lying in the prone position.

Which was impossible. She was no longer in Kandahar. This was Corpus Christi, and they weren't at war here. They were at a wedding. She shook her head and squeezed her eyes closed. When she reopened them, the glint at the top of the building was gone. The long shadow in the sand dune, however, hadn't moved. Not even a little. Okay, so it was probably driftwood.

I'm totally losing my mind. Emma forced her attention back to the happy couple standing in front of her. They were in the middle of exchanging their vows. Moments later, a muffled gunshot made Emma jump.

Again, Lincoln's hand tightened comfortingly on her arm. He leaned in to whisper. "Just a car backfiring."

She stiffened, although she knew he meant well.

I'm not some ravaged soldier suffering from PTSD, for crying out loud! He knew as well as she did that was no car backfiring.

The sound of a second shot made his head whip up.

Yeah, you hear it, too, Officer Hudson, don't you?

Just as Clara and Owen's wedding ceremony was drawing to a close, sirens screamed in the distance. Then the lights of first responder vehicles flickered into view. Men in uniform leaped out of unmarked police cars and converged on the building where she'd first seen what she thought was the glint of a rifle.

There was a knowing grin plastered to Owen's face as he turned his bride around to face their friends. "I warned Clara it would be exciting to marry a Marine," he joked. "I just didn't expect the fireworks to start this soon."

As if on cue, a shower of lights erupted from a lone yacht that had been drifting about a quarter mile off shore. It was the start of a stunning display of fireworks over the water. The fireworks quickly recaptured the attention of their guests, who ooh'd and ah'd over the gorgeous splashes of light against the darkening sky.

Only Emma continued to glance behind them at the growing number of emergency vehicles. A stretcher was removed from an ambulance and swiftly rolled into the building.

"Hey, relax!" Lincoln loosely slung an arm around her shoulders, more or less forcing her to watch the fireworks instead of the mayhem. "We're off duty tonight." He grinned down at her. "Whatever is going on back there is someone else's problem."

She nodded, but she was a little irritated by the way his broad shoulder was blocking her view. Something felt off about the whole situation. Something she couldn't quite put her finger on. Turning her head sideways, she squinted toward the sand dune. The long, dark shadow she thought she'd seen before was completely gone.

A shiver of coldness vibrated through her, as the realization sank in that someone or something had been out there only minutes ago. She was sure of it, and there were ways to prove it. Men lying in the prone left evidence. The divots where a tripod had once rested, footprints, or...something.

The wedding party moved back to the beach house for the reception on the wide, back balcony. White party lights had been strung through the rafters of the cabana stretched over the pool. Bridesmaids and groomsmen slipped inside to change. They returned to the deck in swimsuits and trunks. It was the most fun and relaxed wedding reception Emma had ever attended.

Except for the flash of emergency vehicles next door and the way Lincoln continued to hover over her. Normally, Emma would have appreciated her friend's attentiveness – the way he brought her a chilled beverage and filled a plate of light refreshments for them to share. He was a perfect gentleman and the perfect date for the right gal when she finally came along. But Emma most definitely was not the right gal for him.

Her heart was solidly stuck on one channel. Marcus Zane. Maybe he was nothing more than a ghost, like Clara claimed. Maybe Emma would eventually find a way to move on. Just not tonight.

The combination of wedding vows, a spectacular sunset, and soft music playing in the background had drenched the evening in romance. It was inevitable that powerful memories of her one virtual kiss with Marcus would be stirred.

On a sigh of resignation, she turned to Lincoln. "I think I'm ready to go change." She was careful not to promise to return in a swimsuit. The fact that he would assume that's what she meant was, well, unfortunate. Maybe some other lovely bridesmaid would claim his attention when she failed to return.

Lincoln nodded, eyeing her with concern. "Going to get some rest?"

Okay, so she hadn't fooled him, after all. He knew she wasn't returning.

She nodded and found herself blinking back tears at his kind intuition. "Thank you. For everything. You've been really great."

He winked at her. "I'm the best. Just ask Clara."

They shared a chuckle.

To her dismay, he reached for her hand and toyed a few seconds with her fingers. "Hey, listen, I know things haven't been easy on you since you've been back. Just know we're here for you, alright? Clara, Tinsley, and me. Always."

"Thanks." She gently withdrew her hand from his, wishing things could have been different between them. Maybe in a world without Marcus... But, no. She didn't want to think about a world without him in it.

She could feel Lincoln's gaze on her shoulder blades as she fled for the interior of the beach house. Making her way to the guest room she was sharing with three other bridesmaids, she yanked open her suitcase. After a short debate, she removed her bridesmaid dress and donned a pair of cut-off jean shorts. Though she wasn't in the mood for a swim, they were still staying on the beach. She drew a light hoodie over a tank top to protect against the coastal breezes.

Plus, it gave her a few pockets to stuff things in. She tucked away a flashlight, a tube of lip gloss, and — out of sheer habit — her pistol, which she rarely went anywhere without. Petite, single women couldn't be too careful, especially when they were planning on snooping alone through an isolated sand dune.

Opting to remain barefoot, she padded silently down the stairs. Nodding at a cluster of chattering bridesmaids, she waited until they moved up the stairs before letting herself out the front door. Using the front entrance was the only way to avoid the wedding party in full swing out back.

Pulling up her hood, she jammed her hands in her pockets and lowered her head as she moved to the nearest boardwalk. It was growing dark fast, so it was easy to make herself scarce in the shadows. Instead of heading straight for the sand dunes, however, she lingered several minutes to watch the goings-on at the resort next door.

The police had taped off an area of the parking lot, and forensics experts were combing their way through a dark SUV. Parked beside the taped off area was a car marked Coroner. *Interesting*. And a little gruesome. Had someone died there tonight?

Having seen enough, Emma thoughtfully made her way down the boardwalk to the beach. Whether it was her exhaustion at work or something else, she still couldn't shake the ominous feeling inside her. It was probably completely foolish of her to be outside alone like this with a full-blown police investigation broiling next door.

However, Emma hadn't survived eight years in the Marines on Twizzlers and pixie dust. She possessed the training and instincts of a soldier, and right now her instincts were telling her that there was something worth investigating on the sand dune.

There were a few beachcombers milling at the water's edge, so at least she had the added security of not being alone. She waited until she reached the sand dune before snapping on her flashlight. She didn't just blast it right away, either. She pressed it against the fabric of her pocket, so it only emitted a faint glow.

Then she slowly traversed the sand dune, working her way across broken seashells and prickly tumbleweeds to the place where she thought she'd seen the long piece of driftwood. Or a man.

Her heartbeat sped. Right before her eyes was the evidence she'd been seeking. Footprints. Or rather, boot prints. Man-sized ones.

Emma caught her breath. With a shaking hand, she removed the flashlight from her pocket and directed its full beam at the sand.

For a second, she was crouched above the boot prints. In the next second, however, strong hands caught her shoulders and flipped her to her back in the sand. Her flashlight rolled and snapped off.

"Omigosh!" Emma gasped. "Who's there?"

The hard barrel of a gun was pressed against her rib cage, making her freeze in alarm.

"Don't fight me, Emma. Please."

It was a voice she'd never expected to hear again. Lightheadedness slammed into her so powerfully that, for a split second, she wavered between consciousness and unconsciousness.

"Are you alright, beautiful? I didn't mean to toss you so hard." Remorse thickened his voice, and the cold bite of metal disappeared from her side.

She shivered as his very welcome, very familiar baritone washed over her.

"Marcus?" she rasped, fighting to maintain her lucidity. *Please don't pass out. Please don't pass out.*

"It's me, babe." Warm, gentle hands tugged her to a sitting position. Then they pulled her against a hard chest. "It's me," he repeated against her cheek.

"You're alive," she breathed, sliding her arms around his middle and clinging.

"Yeah. It's a long story," he sighed.

"Everyone said you were gone. That there was no way you could've survive the explosion." Wondering if she was dreaming, she pressed her face to his shoulder, glorying in his strength and nearness, reveling in the faint scent of aftershave laced with ocean breezes.

"There was a ledge not that far down from the cliff's edge."

"Which you didn't know about when you jumped." She fisted her hands in his shirt, torn between dragging him closer and shaking him.

"Correct." His large hands rubbed circles against her back.

So the rumors were true. He'd let go to save Axel

Hammerstone. Her whole body started to tremble. "How come they never found you?" she whispered, hardly able to believe Marcus was present, alive, and wrapped in her embrace.

"Like I said, it's a long story." He tipped her face up to his in the moonlight.

His dark gaze burned into hers, both searching and longing.

As much as she hated any show of weakness, involuntary tears blurred her vision. "I waited, but you never called," she choked.

"Not because I didn't want to." He sounded agonized as he recited her phone number in a low voice. "It's seared into my memory forever. I promise. Just like you are."

"You could've at least found a way to let me know you're still alive!"

"That was kind of hard to do when I'm supposed to be dead."

"You're not making any sense." Tears were streaming hotly down her cheeks by now. Furious tears. Wildly thankful tears. Happy tears. Confused tears.

"Don't cry," he pleaded, cupping her face with both hands.

"I can't help it. You did this to me," she accused damply.

"I know. I'm sorry, Emma. More sorry than you'll

ever know." Then he bent his head to cover her mouth with his.

He was right about one thing. He'd promised months ago that their second kiss would be worth waiting for. He wasn't wrong.

CHAPTER 4: SNIPER IN THE SAND

MARCUS

Months of angst and mental exhaustion disappeared as Emma's warm, soft lips moved eagerly against his.

Marcus could taste her fury mixed with her joy, and he'd never been so happy. Or felt so alive. Their kiss was everything he'd imagined it would be, during the many nights he'd lain awake thinking about her. No, it was more than that. More real, more intense, more heart-shaking.

Throughout all of his planning for the current mission in Corpus Christi, he'd not once considered what he would do if he came face-to-face with Emma Taylor. A reunion between them hadn't been part of the plan. In fact, he could've avoided their encounter, altogether, and probably should have. He'd watched her barefoot approach across the sandy beach through his scope, and had instantly known who it was.

Protocol would have been to pack up and high-tail it back to the rendezvous point to report to his sniper team. But he hadn't wanted to — couldn't quite bring himself to start moving. Over the next several seconds, he'd willed her to walk on past him. It would have been simpler for both of them if she had. And safer.

The other part of him had silently begged her to keep walking his way, to stumble right into him in the sand dune where they could, well...do exactly what they were doing now.

She felt so delicate in his arms, much thinner than when they'd first met. Guilt crashed into him at the knowledge that he probably had something to do with her current state of fragility.

"I'm never going to let you go again," he heard himself growl against the edge of her mouth before diving in for another kiss. He wished like crazy that his bullet-proof vest wasn't between them. He couldn't seem to cuddle her close enough, so he settled for what he could reach. As his hands tangled in the silky strands of her hair, she made a soft sound that went straight to his heart.

He didn't know where his frantic promise had come from, only that he meant every word of it. There was going to be hell to pay when his boss found out about tonight's encounter with Emma, but Marcus didn't care. He was willing to pay whatever price it took to be with the woman of his dreams.

Sure, he believed in his team's mission. And, no, he had no intention of quitting and leaving their ranks. But whatever came next for him was going to have to include her.

If she was willing...

He raised his head to gaze down at her in the moonlight, liking how heavy-lidded and well-kissed she looked. It was a miracle — more than he deserved — that this amazing woman had waited nearly three months for him.

He pushed back her hood, so that her beach-blonde hair tumbled around her shoulders, glistening like white gold. For a moment, all he could do was drink in the feminine curve of her cheeks and her brown eyes that seemed to glow from an inner light. *Man!* She was so beautiful that it made his heart ache.

"I'm in love with you, Emma." Since everything he cared about had been stripped from him in recent months, he'd learned not to take anything for granted. Or anyone. Which meant there was only room for truth between them — the whole truth and nothing but the truth.

She gave a knowing, girlish chuckle. "We barely know each other." Her musical alto surrounded him like a caress, drawing him deeper beneath her spell.

He snorted. "Not true." He knew the details of her life inside and out, right down to the difficulty she had sleeping since her return from her deployment. He pressed his lips to her temple and breathed in deeply. "I know you're an award-winning MP, K9 certified, and a deadly accurate shot with that pistol you have tucked in your sweatshirt. I also know you've served as a bridesmaid in three weddings, attended grief counseling, and haven't gone on a single date since your return from Afghanistan." That last detail really stoked his ego.

Her lips parted in shock. "I'm almost afraid to ask how you know all of that."

He palmed her cheek. "Would you believe me if I told you that knowing these things is part of my current mission?"

She caught her breath. "Which is what, exactly?"

"Helping to protect every Marine who survived the explosion in Kandahar."

"Why me? I wasn't even present when the explosion went off."

"No, but your MP unit processed the scene afterward."

She made a scoffing sound. "Actually, Captain Miller forced me to sit that one out. He assigned me a few back-to-back shifts at our headquarters."

"I'm aware, but our enemies don't know that. They tagged both my Marine unit and yours as loose ends." They'd been picking the hapless Marines off one by one ever since. There'd been a "random" fire in one Marine's apartment building in New Mexico, and a head-on collision with another Marine in Arizona last month by a "drunk" driver. Since it was a hit-and-run and the perp was still at large, the authorities had yet to figure out what was really happening was something far more ominous. There might as well have been crosshairs on the foreheads of every Marine who'd survived the ambush.

"What enemies?" Emma shook her head. "I take it we're no longer talking about those who oppose the peace keeping troops in Afghanistan?"

"Correct. I'm talking about the fact that our unit bumbled its way into a war zone between two major arms traffickers on our trip to Kandahar."

Her expression registered more fury than surprise. "How convenient," she shot back dryly, "considering the number of military weapons and vehicles you were transporting — not to mention one very important prisoner of war."

He found her ability to quickly connect the dots both impressive and wildly hot. Tracing her lower lip with the pad of his thumb, he muttered, "Agreed. The folks I'm currently working for think it may have been an inside job." All evidence was certainly pointing in that direction. Meaning, they most likely had a dirty pocket of soldiers on the take. Men in uniform who'd sold out the safety of their comrades for a price.

Emma leaned into his touch and splayed her hand against his heart. Or rather, over his bulletproof vest that rested against his heart. "Does this mean you're no longer a Marine?"

He reached up to cover her hand with his own. "On paper, I'm a dead Marine," he reminded.

"Technically, you're still listed as MIA." There was a catch in her voice that tugged every one of his heart strings.

For the time being, anyway. "True," he concurred softly. "But they're considering switching my status to KIA, so they can pay out my life insurance proceeds."

"Oh, Marcus!" she gasped. Her lovely brown gaze turned stricken. "What about your family? Don't they deserve to know the truth?"

"Trust me when I say this. I hate everything I've had to put them through since the explosion." He clenched his jaw. "But their belief that I'm gone is actually what is keeping them safe. Maybe someday I'll be at liberty to rise from the dead and bare my soul to them, but not now."

"Why did you tell me, then?"

"I wasn't going to," he confessed, dropping his arms. "Every ounce of logic was hollering that I shouldn't."

She searched his face. "What changed your mind?"

"You, sweetheart." He groaned and ran a hand over his face. "It nearly killed me to see you on that dude's arm at the wedding earlier. Not that you didn't have every right to move on with your life in my absence. Then when I looked up a few minutes ago and saw you heading my way, it was like fate was giving me a second chance to make things right with you. And, well, even a Marine's willpower has its limits."

"So you think I'm your sweetheart?" she teased.

"I want you to be," he returned fervently, reaching for her hand again. "More than anything." He drew a deep breath. "Don't get me wrong. I believe in what I'm doing for a living these days. It's a cause I had no problem pledging my life to." He frowned and shook his head. "I just don't want to do it alone, anymore." His mind skidded over the possibilities and landed on the only one that made sense. The only idea with a shot at keeping her in his life.

"How can we ever be together?" Her blonde brows rose. "You're a ghost, Marcus."

"By marrying me." Since they were seated in the sand, trying to avoid detection from any passers-by, it didn't make sense to take a knee in front of her. However, he was very much on his knees inside his heart and head.

"Marry you?" she squeaked. "Where would we live? What would we do?" She shook her head, looking perplexed. "You haven't exactly been forthcoming with the details about your current position."

"Sorry." He gave a self-deprecatory chuckle. "I thought it was obvious. I'm part of a special operations task force, babe. They recruited me the same day they rescued me off that ledge."

"You mean special forces, like the Raiders?"

"Not exactly. It's something new. Something more off the books. And I think they'd jump at the opportunity to add a woman of your training and experience to the team."

"Marcus," she whispered, sounding both awed and stricken. "I have responsibilities I'm not in the position to simply walk away from. Unlike you, my family and friends are under the distinct impression that I'm alive."

He knew what he said next was going to be crucial if he wanted to make her a permanent fixture in his life. "True, but they're very accustomed to you coming and going from their lives, babe. You could be gone for weeks, or even months, and they wouldn't question it. All it would really require is a change in job description."

She gave a huff of surprise. "So you're asking me to live a double life?" Though she looked doubtful, she hadn't outright turned him down. Yet. That was something.

"What I'm mainly asking you to do is marry me." He lifted her hand to his lips.

"Marry you!" she gasped again. "Seriously?"

"And join me in the world of covert operations, because I'm in love with you, and every instinct in me is telling me you have feelings for me in return."

"You know that I do."

Her declaration made his heart sing. "You sure kiss like you do."

Though her color deepened in the shadows, indicating she was blushing, her smile turned mischievous. "So what would an undercover wife for an undercover operative do, anyway?"

Her question took his breath away. Any doubts he might've had about the wisdom of his impromptu marriage proposal vanished. She was very much up to the challenge of being his woman. His perfect partner.

He grinned back. "How about I introduce you to my team, and we find out together?"

"When?"

"Tomorrow. I'll set it up and call you on this after I do." He dug in the pocket of his dark cargo pants and unearthed a phone, which he pressed into her hand. Curling her fingers around it, he explained, "It's a burner phone."

"Thanks." To his delight, she accepted it without batting an eyelash and tucked it inside the back pocket of her jean cutoffs.

He gazed at her for an extended moment before speaking again, feeling drunk with happiness. "Does this mean we're engaged?"

Her eyes went all soft and vulnerable at his question. "Yes."

There was only one appropriate response to that.

He drew her back into his embrace and sealed his mouth over hers.

IF THERE WAS SUCH a thing as being delirious from joy, Emma fit the description. Never before had she waffled between laughter and tears so many times in such a short period.

Marcus's kisses were both tender and possessive, cherishing yet demanding. He was hers. Her man, her protector, her real live American hero.

"Emma," he finally groaned, lifting his head. "You're going to have to be the stronger one here — strong enough to get up and walk away from me, because I don't think I have it in me to let you go ever again." Whether intentionally or involuntarily, his arms tightened fiercely around her.

"I'm not near ready to let you go, either." She untwined one arm from around his neck, so she could trace the angle of his jaw. "I think I fell in love with you the moment we met."

The breath whooshed out of his chest at her unexpected admission. He turned his face to kiss her finger. "Any particular reason?"

"No. To this day, I have no idea what it was about you — only that I was drawn to you before you ever approached me and started talking. It was the way you were looking at me, I guess. All I could think was that my heart was in serious trouble."

"Same." He gave her a crooked smile. "Despite the way the guys were forever teasing me about being a player, I definitely wasn't on the prowl the day we were heading to Kandahar. I was too busy dealing with the security of the prisoner we were transporting. Then, in the midst of my concerns, I looked up, saw you for the first time, and boom. I knew. You were the one."

The one. They were the two most precious words anyone had ever spoken to Emma, two words made even more special by months of grieving, being apart from him, and longing for a phone call she didn't think would ever come.

Her cell phone buzzed with an incoming message. "Sorry, but I should probably see who it is." Inwardly bemoaning the interruption, she disengaged herself from Marcus's arms to reach inside the hand warmer pocket of her hoodie. She withdrew her phone and frowned over her growing list of messages.

Her most recent text was from Lincoln. *Where are you? Everyone's worried about you.*

She sighed as she read it. "Apparently, my absence has been noticed. Guess I better get back before my friends send out a search party."

Marcus's dark brows rose. "You mean blondie is missing you," he noted dryly.

"Something like that." She grinned. "Why? Are you jealous?"

"Should I be?"

"No." She met his gaze squarely. "I'm assuming you know everything about him already, right down to his badge number, so I'll get right to the good stuff. Yes, he would like for there to be more between us, but it never happened. We've known each other most of our lives, so I think it would have happened a long time ago if it was meant to be. As it turns out, you're what was meant to be, Marcus. You're just going to have to trust me on that."

"I do." The look in his eyes took her breath away.

"Good." She gave him a tremulous smile. "What you're asking of me is...huge. It's going to take a whole lot of trust on both of our parts to make this work."

"I know, babe." He gave a huff of wonder. "It means everything to me that you're willing to give us a chance." He shook his head. "I just wish we had more time to date first. What I wouldn't give to take you dining and dancing, to romance you the way you deserve."

She hastily typed a response to Lincoln. *Went for a walk. On my way back.* Then she tucked her phone away. "Marcus..." She caught his gorgeous gaze again. "Like you, I've kissed my fair share of frogs. Enough of them to know that it's not about the dinner or the dance. It's about who you're with." She reached for him one last time, hating the necessity of saying goodbye. Again.

His arms came hungrily around her, and she melted against him. "You're the only guy I've ever waited by the phone for."

"Thank you." He dipped his head to brush his mouth tenderly against hers.

"You're not my first marriage proposal, either," she continued, "but you're the only one I said yes to. The only one I even considered saying yes to."

"Making me the luckiest guy on the planet." This time he deepened their kiss, rendering her breathless.

"I want to be with you, Marcus. If that means joining a special ops team so that we can be together, then so be it, because you make me happy."

"My newest, most important mission is to keep you that way," he promised, touching his forehead to hers. "Forever and always."

"I don't want to say goodbye." There was a catch to her voice. What if something else happened to him after she returned to the beach house — something that would keep them apart again indefinitely? She couldn't bear the thought.

"Then don't." He slowly raised his head. "Just keep being strong for me, babe."

"I will." She playfully flicked a finger at his shoulder, forcing down the lump of emotion in her throat. "So long as you keep your word and call me this time."

He nodded. "Tell me you love me again before you go."

"I love you, Marcus."

He held out his hands, palms facing her. "I love you, too, Emma."

She pressed her hands to his and marveled at how beautiful they looked together — her smaller, lighter ones against his larger, darker ones. Then she stood on legs that trembled. Without another word, she forced herself to start walking across the sand toward the beach house.

In the event anyone was watching her, she didn't look back. However, she knew Marcus had his scope trained on her. Though she hadn't asked, she knew he would continue to stand vigil over her and keep her safe throughout the night. And tomorrow he would call. Just the thought of hearing his voice again made her giddy with excitement.

Gosh, it was a spectacular night! How hadn't she noticed it before? The moon was full, the sky was studded with stars, and her heart was brimming with happiness. Laughter and voices were still ringing out, and the round white party lights were still shining brightly on the back deck, assuring her that the wedding reception remained in full swing. She reached the stairs and skipped nimbly up them, feeling like she was floating.

"There you are!" Lincoln met her at the top of the stairs, a scowl painted across his well-defined features.

"Here I am," she sang out with such an inane sounding giggle that she clapped a hand over her mouth to muffle it.

"I thought you were tired." His gaze narrowed suspiciously on her face.

"I am." She lowered her hand. "As usual, though, I couldn't sleep." She waved at the sky. "I was hoping a dose of moonlight would do the trick."

"So you went out alone and unarmed," he growled. "In the dark."

"I'm never unarmed, my friend." She patted the pocket of her hoodie. "I'm not the kind of gal you or anyone else needs to worry about."

His scowl deepened. "I care about you, Emma. Is that a crime?" He fell into step beside her as she skirted the pool.

Several guests were seated on the tile deck, holding plates and beverages and trailing their feet in the water. A few of them waved their glasses and called out greetings.

She waved back, then turned her face up to Lincoln's so she could wrinkle her nose at him. "No, it's not a crime. So long as you don't do something stupid to ruin a lifelong friendship."

He glared. "Just for the record, I've never asked you out."

She hated the knowledge that she was hurting his feelings, but she was engaged to Marcus now and likely to be married soon. Lincoln Hudson was, quite simply, too important to her to keep him emotionally dangling. She waited until they ducked past the sliding glass door before she finished saying her piece.

"I care for you, too, Lincoln. I always have and always will. That's why I want to be perfectly honest with you about...everything. I know it looks like I'm a single gal, but I'm not. I fell in love with someone while I was overseas, and I'm not over him yet." *I don't plan to ever get over him.*

"Fair enough." His upper lip curled. "Now let me be equally honest. Number one: By strict definition, you *are* single."

Her heart sank. *No, I'm not. Not by any definition, my friend. I'm just not at liberty to set things straight with you on the topic.*

"Number two: I respect the fact that your heart belongs to someone else. For now, anyway." They reached the stairs, and he stepped smoothly in front of her, blocking her way up. "Number three: I'm single, too, and I'm very interested in dating you when you become available again. I'm sorry if that's not what you wanted to hear from me this weekend, but..." His smile didn't reach his eyes. "Like you said, we're being honest with each other."

"I'm flattered, Lincoln. I really am, but—"

"Good." He smirked. "You should be, because I'm pretty awesome."

She swallowed a chuckle, not wanting to encourage him. "You are, and you're going to make some amazing woman really happy someday." *I just happen to not be that woman.*

His chin jutted stubbornly. "I've already met an amazing woman, and I'm not in any rush to go find another one."

"Okay, well, I'm not asking you to go hold up a sign on the street." She made a face at him. "I just don't want you waiting for me."

"That's not your decision to make."

She drummed her fingers on the stair railing post. "Lincoln, I'm really tired."

"You don't look it." However, he moved sideways to make room for her to pass. "You did earlier, but not anymore. Something's different about you." His gaze turned speculating.

Uh-oh. Though her heart fluttered in alarm, she forced a smirk to her lips. "Thank you for noticing. I think the bazillions of stars out tonight helped put me back in touch with my inner peace."

To her relief, his hard mouth relaxed into a faint smile. "I like the sound of that."

"Me, too." Before he could say anything else, she brushed past him to dance up the stairs. "'Night, Lincoln!" she called and gave a flutter of her hand over her shoulder.

"Goodnight, Emma," he returned quietly. She could feel his gaze on her back as she reached the top of the stairs and rounded the corner.

The moment she entered her guest room, she was pounced on by a bridesmaid named Cecilia.

"Omigosh!" the pert-nosed brunette gushed. "I'd recognize that look a mile away. Who is he?"

Emma frowned, not following her. "Who is who?"

"The guy you kissed. Come on! I can tell." The woman gave a bounce of excitement on her bunk. "Details, details!"

Am I seriously that transparent? A shiver of delicious apprehension worked its way through Emma's shoulder blades. "I have no idea what you're talking about," she lied. "All I did was take a solo walk on the beach."

"Uh-huh." Cecilia didn't sound the least convinced. "Was it Lincoln Hudson? Everyone can see the way he looks at you."

Rolling her eyes, Emma plopped down on the lower bunk across from the other woman's bed and stretched out. "I'm so tired, I could seriously hibernate until spring." She closed her eyes, jamming her hands in the pocket of her hoodie and closing her fingers around the burner phone from Marcus.

"Fine. You don't want to talk about it. I can take a hint." Her roommate sounded a bit miffed, but it couldn't be helped. "Party pooper!" she hissed before she made her exit and shut the door a little harder than necessary behind her.

Emma was relieved she was gone. *Marcus is going to call me this time! He's finally going to call me, Lord willing that nothing else prevents him from doing so.* Cradling the phone against her belly, she felt herself slipping into honest-to-gosh sleep for the first time in months.

CHAPTER 5: THE ASSET

MARCUS

Marcus watched as Officer Lincoln Hudson accosted Emma the moment she arrived at the pool deck. He could tell by the guy's body language that he definitely wanted to be more than friends. Clenching his jaw in frustration, Marcus mentally replayed her words to drown out the stab of jealousy at what he was having to witness.

It's going to take a whole lot of trust on both of our parts to make this work.

It was going to take a lot of love, too. *Man!* As he studied his lovely fiancée in action, it was clear to him that she was doing her part to maintain some clear boundaries between herself and Lincoln. She leaned slightly away from him when glancing in his direction. Plus, she wasn't pausing or stopping to extend their chitchat. She kept moving.

Only after she disappeared inside the beach

house with his competition, did Marcus flip his earpiece back on.

"A6 reporting. Target safely inside." Even though they were on a secure channel, they never used their real names.

Digby MacLamore's rumble of laughter filled his ear. "Copy that. Nice stretch of radio silence there, Romeo. You do realize I've been on my scope the entire time."

Marcus's heart sank. He knew it was Dig's way of telling him he'd seen him with Emma. "Really? I figured you took a detour to Fiji to soak up some rays."

"Listen, man. I'm really happy for the two of you, but what are you going to do about her?"

"Marry her and bring her on board as an asset, if the powers-that-be are willing." There was no point in lying. Not only was Dig one of his closest friends, he was a soldier Marcus respected enormously.

"You're not exactly giving them a choice."

"No."

"A risky move." The bleakness in Dig's voice was a reminder that Dig, himself, was a married man. A father, too, of a tiny infant named John Tyler, or JT as his family had taken to calling him. He'd been born prematurely during their deployment, making Dig desperate to get back home. "What if they say no?"

"Like you pointed out, I'm not exactly giving

them a choice." He'd allowed Emma to overtake his position and thereby compromise their entire operation, if anyone decided to play hardball with the situation. He was banking on the fact that their boss would see her as a useful ally, instead. "With the election only a little over a month away, we need all the help we can get." Marcus, Dig, and the rest of their team were literally working around the clock to complete their mission, so they could finally return home to be reunited with their families.

"It's both of our hides you're playing Russian roulette with here."

Yeah, it was, and Marcus was well aware they were about to have those same hides handed back to them. He knew Dig wouldn't flicker so much as an eyelash when it happened, either. That was how solid of a friend he was.

MARCUS AND DIG pulled guard for the rest of the night and were relieved from duty by a second pair of snipers at daybreak. Packing up their gear, they returned to the rendezvous point, where they were swiftly and heatedly debriefed.

A vein in Colonel Peterson's temple throbbed as he unleashed the full brunt of his fury on them. "Give me one good reason why I shouldn't send you both up the chain to be tried for war crimes."

Maybe because we have the moral high ground here, and you know it. Marcus and Dig were standing at attention within the narrow confines of their subterranean meet-up. It was a well concealed cavern, high on a ridge overlooking the bay.

Marcus studied their boss, opting not to defend Dig. There was no point in claiming he'd forced his friend's complicity on the matter. They were all professional snipers here. All responsible for their own actions.

"She'll make a powerful asset, sir. As you are aware, she's a Marine with eight years of MP experience, K9 certified, and an expert marksman."

The colonel's upper lip curled. "I reckon those are your only reasons for compromising our mission?"

Did I? The way Marcus saw it, he'd just made their position stronger. He was a God, family, country kinda guy — in that order. If his boss couldn't see that, then he'd recruited the wrong Marine for their current special task force. "I believe you just yesterday mentioned you were desperate for an extra uniform in San Antonio. A police officer with her experience would be perfect for the job." That was where the military sent most of their burn victims.

Two particular Marines, who were very near and dear to his heart — Sergeant Axel Hammerstone and Sergeant Hunt Ryker — were currently undergoing treatments at the burn center there. They were going to require a protection detail throughout their long road to recovery, especially after they were medically boarded out of the service due to the extensive wounds they'd sustained in battle.

"I don't recall recruitment being part of your MOS, soldier."

MOS stood for military occupational specialty code, a fancy name for *job description*. The truth was, Marcus's job description was a little murky these days, and they both knew it. He gave an inward shrug and went for the money shot. "I had a narrow window of opportunity, sir, and went for it. Just like you trained me to."

Colonel Peterson's expression waffled between apoplexy and humor. The humor won out. "At ease!" he barked.

Marcus and Dig relaxed their positions with a wary side glance at each other.

Mark Peterson flicked a hand in the air. "Oh, for Pete's sake, start cleaning your weapons!"

Marcus hastily bent to unzip his pack and start disassembling his equipment. Dig mirrored his movements. "I gave her my burner phone, sir. She's expecting a call this morning." He briefly closed his eyes. *Please don't make me stand her up again.*

Colonel Peterson rounded on him and threw up his hands. "What am I missing here?" Since Emma Taylor was one of the targets they were protecting, he already knew her personnel file inside and out. "How in the heck did one petite female manage to compromise the position of one of my best Marines?"

Marcus bristled. "She's a Marine, too, sir."

Something in his expression must have given away the truth, because the colonel groaned and rubbed a hand through his silver buzz cut. "You have got to be kidding me! This isn't about being a Marine, is it? Your feelings are involved." He paced the small cavern. "I can personally vouch for the fact you were single and unattached when we shipped out. When exactly did you fall for this woman?"

"Minutes before the explosion, sir. MP checkpoint in Kandahar."

"I'm still not following the how," his commander gritted out.

Marcus shrugged. He was still trying to figure that out for himself. "One glance," he muttered. "That's all it took, sir."

His commander rounded on him, face turning red. "Are you seriously expecting me to swallow this love-at-first-sight load of crap? We aren't living inside some chick flick, Sergeant Zane. This is war."

A war against corruption at the highest levels of the military and government, no less. They'd just finished uncovering the smoking gun they needed to expose a senator who appeared to be profiting from the arms trafficking. Since he was up for re-election, they were going to time the press release bomb to explode in approximately two weeks. Unfortunately, this would only be the beginning of the fight. There could be, and most likely were, more officials involved. The colonel's special task force was working closely with a team of CIA agents to follow the money trail. So far, their investigation had been stonewalled by foreign banks managing offshore accounts. If their team pulled enough threads, however, the evidence would eventually unravel. Or so they hoped.

Marcus laid the pieces of his weapon in a neat row on the cavern floor. "She's an asset we can't afford to pass over, sir."

"You say that like you don't have me backed into a very difficult corner, sergeant."

Marcus wisely maintained his silence.

After another groan of irritation, Colonel Peterson finally made his decision. "Make the call and bring her here at nightfall. Blindfolded."

"Yes, sir." Marcus shot Dig an incredulous look. Dig merely shrugged. Though Marcus had been hoping like crazy, neither of them had been expecting such a quick capitulation on the part of their commander.

He grabbed a few hours of sleep on his bedroll in the back of the cavern. Then he went to work. The first order of business was his all-important phone call to Emma.

She didn't pick up until the fourth ring.

"Are you alone, beautiful?" he asked softly. He was strolling the water's edge in camouflage swim trunks and an olive t-shirt. A tan ball cap was pulled low over his sunglasses to provide a bit of anonymity.

"I am now."

"Any interest in meeting me at the Oceanview boat rental dock at eight?"

"Very interested." Her voice held a shy note.

"It's an initial interview with no guarantees, but I have a good feeling about it." Colonel Peterson hadn't gotten to where he was by misreading people. He was crusty around the edges, but he was solid on the inside. He would surely be able to see that what Emma had to offer their team was pure gold.

"How should I dress?"

"To make an impression. You'll get one shot."

"It's a date." She sounded more amused than nervous, which he found super hot.

"I love you."

"You better," she teased, "because I'm ditching a ladies' night out for you."

"I'll make it worth your while, sweetheart." He disconnected the line.

EMMA KNEW she was grinning like an idiot at the burner phone, but she couldn't help it. *Marcus is alive!* She stuffed the phone back inside her pocket and stepped off the sidewalk onto the circle drive leading to the Hudsons' beach house. She'd moved outside to take his call in order to avoid any eavesdroppers.

A few sharp beeps from a car horn made her hop to the edge of the driveway. To her surprise, a cheerful yellow cab rolled toward the beach house. It halted at the front door, and a trio of bridesmaids converged on it with their suitcases. Cecilia was among them. She glanced up and gave Emma a cool nod. Then she joined the laughing, chattering group of women inside the cab.

Emma blinked at them as they drove away. Looked like their ladies' night out was being canceled. *That's weird!* Why hadn't anyone told her? Hurrying back to the house, she was dismayed to find Lincoln waiting on the porch. He was lounged against one of the white columns. Since he hadn't been there before Marcus's call, she suspected he'd purposefully sought her out.

"Sleep well?" he inquired with one blonde brow raised as she reached the stairs. He looked surprisingly ironed and pressed in a pair of tan slacks and a white button-up shirt that wasn't tucked in.

"I did, thank you. And you?"

"Not so much."

She lowered her sunglasses to squint up at him. The tired lines around his eyes made her smile slip. "Why not? What's wrong?"

"I'm worried, Emma." He eyed her somberly as she mounted the bottom rung of the stairs.

"About," she prodded, leaning the heels of her sneakers off the edge of the stair to stretch her calves. She was wearing black running shorts and a neon pink rayon hoodie. Her hair was scrunched back in a ponytail.

"You."

"Okay. You have my attention." *Please, don't turn this into another awkward moment for both of us.*

"No, I don't, which is making it really hard for me to look after you in my sister's absence." Clara and Owen had hopped a plane to Bora Bora late last night to begin their honeymoon.

Emma snickered. "That sounds like Clara." The sly, interfering matchmaker side of her. "You don't have to do everything your older sister says, you know. Out of sight, out of mind," she sang out teasingly.

"That would be easier if the resort next door hadn't reported a homicide."

Her jaw dropped. "A what?"

He nodded grimly. "Remember all those emergency vehicles circling like hawks last night?"

She nodded, frowning.

"Well, it wasn't over a simple gas leak. Somebody was shot. They're keeping it out of the press, but I have a friend in the FBI, and—"

"The FBI!" She gaped in amazement at him.

"Yeah." He glance around them and lowered his voice. "The stiff has ties to a state senator, who just happens to be under investigation for a few irregular campaign contributions."

"Ouch." Her insides chilled at the reminder that Marcus had been hunched beside a sniper rifle in the sand dune last night.

"Typical politician problems." He waved a hand dismissively. "I'm more worried about the sniper rifle they found in the guy's room."

"No way!" Another sniper?

"Unfortunately," he sighed. "It was trained on the west strand of the beach."

Her stomach started to hurt. "At us? This house is on the west strand, Lincoln."

"Hard to say, but I'm not any more thrilled about the possibilities than you are." He pushed away from the column he'd been leaning against. "To play it safe, I'm sending everyone home early."

"Smart, though I'm kinda shattered over the thought of missing ladies' night out."

"Yeah, you look pretty shattered." He chuckled knowingly, though his expression remained worried.

"Guess I better go pack." Her thoughts were already jumping ahead to her interview, which wasn't scheduled to take place until eight o'clock. Though it might be her only shot at impressing

Marcus's boss, they were going to have to risk his ire by moving it up.

"Really?" Lincoln drawled. "Because you have a roommate claiming you never unpacked in the first place."

"That's mostly true." She smiled tightly as she swept past Lincoln up the stairs. "It would be more accurate to say I pack light." Gosh, he was being nosy, all of a sudden!

"Want to hitch a ride with me back to Dallas?" he called after her.

Emma gave an inward groan at the reminder that she'd ridden down with Clara and Tinsley. *He's going to think I'm crazy if I say no.* She paused in the doorway. "Sure, but I have to run an errand first, Officer Hudson. It'll take me about an hour, so if you're in a hurry to hit the road..."

"I'll wait for you."

Of course you will. Biting her lip, she nodded.

"Need a sidekick for that errand?"

"I'm already allowing you to babysit me on the ride back home," she shot back. "Don't push your luck." She pushed open the front door and took the second-story stairs two at a time.

Since she had the guest room to herself now, she flipped on the exhaust fan in the restroom to provide a bit of white noise. Then she dialed Marcus on his burner phone.

He picked up right away. "Hey, there, beautiful."

"We need to move up the interview," she informed him flatly. "Apparently, there was a homicide last night at the resort next door, so the Hudson's are sending everyone home early."

"Can't you kill time at an ice cream shop or something?"

"Lincoln has offered to drive me home, and it'll only raise his suspicions if I turn him down. We leave in an hour."

"I'll see what I can arrange."

"Marcus, I'm heading to the boat rental now." He needed to understand she was serious about moving the interview.

"Copy that, sweetheart."

As she disconnected the line, she stared down at her outfit in dismay. So much for dressing to impress! There was no time to change. She knelt to slide a blade inside the hidden holster of her left sneaker. Then she grabbed her pistol and tucked it in the back waistband of her shorts. After a moment of hesitation, she swapped out her neon pink shirt for one the shade of eggplant and jammed a matching ballcap over her ponytail.

Knowing Lincoln was probably hovering somewhere nearby, she was sure to make plenty of noise while opening the sliding glass door and clattering her way across the pool deck. Noise sounded more innocuous than stealth and was less likely to be questioned by her police officer friend.

In case he was still watching, she ducked through the front entrance of a beachside cafe and made a beeline for the side entrance. If Lincoln decided to follow her, that would slow him down. Then she traversed her way across a boardwalk and continued down the busy sidewalk running along the street front.

Fortunately, Mikey's Boat Rental was only a few blocks down from the Hudsons. To Emma's delight and amazement, Marcus had arrived ahead of her. He was at the front counter, renting a speed boat from the sound of things.

Emma wasn't sure if she was supposed to recognize or ignore him in public, so she waited for him to give her a cue.

He spun around with the boat keys in hand. "There you are, babe!"

One glance at his swim trunks and olive t-shirt told her she might have accidentally worn the right outfit for the occasion, after all.

Gliding in his direction, she leaned in to air kiss his cheek. "Sorry I'm late," she gushed. "My sisters insisted on a shopping excursion to La Palmera this morning. I knew it would be cutting it close, but, you know...sisters."

The guy at the counter gave an understanding snort. "Sounds like my wife." He shoved a handful of his longish, sun-bleached hair behind one ear.

Then the door chimed, announcing another

customer. "Dock four behind the shack," he mumbled distractedly to them and shot a winning smile to the newcomer. "Welcome to Mikey's!"

Marcus bent to nuzzle Emma's cheek as he opened the door for her. "Well played," he muttered in her ear. "You're a natural at this." He splayed a hand across her lower back and undoubtedly noted the bulge of her pistol.

She smiled, wanting nothing more than to tug his head down for a kiss.

"Please tell me you're necking with me inside your head again," he begged softly as they made their way across the sunny pier to dock four.

"I can't tell you all of my secrets!" She pretended indignation.

Their speed boat was all gassed up and ready to go. Marcus revved the motor and slowly backed the craft away from the pier. Moments later, they careened away from the shoreline and headed for deeper bay waters.

She tipped her head back, enjoying the kiss of the sun on her skin. Once they were a mile or so out, however, she tossed aside her sunglasses and hat to drink in the sight of her fiancé standing at the wheel. The dark outline of a young woman's face with flowing hair was inked across one bulging bicep.

Emma laughed and angled her head at his tat. "Dare I ask?" She had to raise her voice to be heard against the sound of the motor and the wind.

He cut their speed before answering. "It's my sister, Kiera. Long story short, she was a miracle baby. I had the sleeve commissioned in case I ever needed to be reminded of miracles."

"A guy with a soft spot for his baby sister? Wow!" She shook her head in bemusement. "If I wasn't already in love with you..." she sighed.

He abruptly flipped off the ignition, allowing them to drift toward a secluded inlet. The ridge ahead of them parted like a V, revealing a small, sandy beachhead. "Say that again, sweetheart." He joined her on the white vinyl seat and gathered her close.

"I love you," she whispered, "so much."

"I'll never get tired of hearing it." He claimed her mouth and showed her just how much her words meant to him.

For several breathless moments, it was just him and her while the rest of the world disappeared. Then she felt a length of cloth cover her eyes.

He deftly tied it behind her head. "Still trust me?"

"I do," she assured. The blindfold meant they were getting close to their destination.

A few minutes later, their boat bumped lightly against something solid. He guided her from the craft, and they walked from the squishy turf at the water's edge to a rocky, uneven surface Then it quickly became darker and cooler. Her guess was that they'd entered a tunnel or a cave.

"Remove her blindfold," a gravelly voice barked.

She found herself blinking in solid blackness. She waved her hand directly in front of her face and couldn't see it. Seconds later, a lantern flashed on, and the face of a middle aged man appeared. "The sniper at the resort was targeting you and Owen Banks," he announced without preamble. "My team neutralized him and saved your life."

"Thank you, sir." His precise movements and authoritative manner told her that she was in the presence of a military officer, which meant Marcus was still in the Marines. She liked that fact. "How can I help keep the rest of our unit safe?"

His forehead wrinkled a fraction, the only tell-tale sign that she'd surprised him. "We have two Marines at a burn unit in San Antonio we could use some assistance watchdogging over. Both had a front seat at the explosion in Kandahar. Someone out there is convinced they saw something they shouldn't have. Something that could implicate a ring of arms traffickers."

Her heart raced with excitement at the knowledge that he was most likely referring to Marcus's friends who'd been airlifted out of Afghanistan. "How soon can you have me on a plane, sir?" she inquired softly.

"As soon as you're married."

She blinked, momentarily speechless.

He guffawed.

"Sergeant Zane is requesting me to send the two of you undercover as a husband and wife team. As harebrained and Hollywood as that sounds, I'm inclined to agree that sending in two Marines will be twice as effective as sending in one. Assuming you accept his marriage proposal, of course."

Her lips twitched. "Already done, sir."

"Good. You'll be assigned to our special task force for your remaining two months in the Marines, during which time you'll report directly to me. I'd recommend you hold dropping your reenlistment paperwork until you're sure this new line of work is the right fit for you."

Meaning he intended for her to prove herself before offering her a more permanent position on his team.

"*Semper fi*, sir," she returned simply.

CHAPTER 6: INCOGNITO

EMMA

Lincoln was tight-lipped for the first few minutes of their drive to Dallas. He glanced over at Emma in the passenger a seat a few times, before finally exploding, "You went sailing? That was your errand?"

"Yes, Mom," she chuckled. Her mind raced for a way to steer their conversation to safer ground. There was no point in denying it. The salt spray on her hoodie was a dead giveaway that she'd been out on the gulf waters.

"Why?"

She scowled playfully at him. "I was kidding about the mom thing. I don't sign in and out with anyone, not even longtime family friends."

He gripped the steering wheel of his navy Land Rover so tightly that his knuckles turned white. "Um...paging Emma Taylor, in case she's left the universe. There's been an open homicide investigation taking place all morning next door, remember?"

"Yes, and life continues for the rest of us, Linc. I'm also going grocery shopping this evening and out for a run in the morning, in case you're wondering."

His glare deepened. "You're kinda missing the point, Em. I'm not trying to curtail your freedom; I'm just trying to keep you safe."

"Not your responsibility." Why couldn't he see that?

"You could've at least let me come with you on your oceanside errand." He made a frustrated sound. "As a friend."

"I didn't need your help this morning. I do, however, need and appreciate your offer to drive me home." She beamed an overly bright smile across the console at him.

"Fine," he sighed. "You don't want me to know where you went."

"Bingo."

"Can you at least assure me that you're okay? Not off to see some specialist for a rare and wasting disease?"

Her laughter pealed around them. "Now that you mention it, I did find a strange set of blue, purple, and pink polka dots running down my right calf this morning."

"Shut up, please."

Gladly. Can we change the subject now?

"Where's Tinsley?" She was a little surprised his younger sister wasn't at least hitching a ride to the airport.

"She caught an early flight. Why?" he demanded sarcastically. "Were you hoping she'd be here to play chaperone?"

"Just making conversation. So...what's next for you, career-wise?" Clara had mentioned something about him being in some sort of transition.

His expression relaxed. "Thanks for asking. Since you seemed to be avoiding me all weekend, I wasn't sure you cared."

Could we please stop with the wounded bear act already? She stuck her tongue out at him. "My ears are all yours for the next..." she glanced down at the screen of her cell phone, "six hours and seven minutes." She arched her brows at him. "Or longer if you stop to feed me."

His lips twitched. "You hungry?"

"Famished, actually." The meeting with Marcus's team had been all cryptic and rushed. Afterward, they'd sent her back alone with the boat to Mikey's.

The tired lines in Lincoln's face seemed to lighten a bit. "What'll it be? Hibachi grill, a steakhouse, or something else?"

She shot him an incredulous look. "Hey, this is Texas, the beef capital of the world. Anything else would be sacrilegious, don't you think?" She could've cared less, but she seemed to remember he was a big steak fan.

He looked pleased. "Saltgrass it is."

He waited until they were seated inside the rustic dining room before diving into his future plans. "I applied for one of those coveted spots at the Texas Hotline Training Center. I assume you've heard of them?"

"Is the sky blue?" She peeked at him over the top of her menu. "It's some of the best training in the world of law enforcement. What certification are you going for?"

"Tracking and scouting."

She nodded in approval. "That sounds similar to the training I received in my dog handler course with the Marines. Where do you see yourself next? On a search and rescue team? Hunting down missing persons?"

"Yes and yes." His blue gaze glinted across the table at her, but he paused when their waitress arrived to take their orders. He snorted when Emma selected a grilled chicken salad.

"Seriously?" He shook his head as their waitress walked away. "You had me take you to a steakhouse, so you could order a salad?"

"No. I would've ordered a salad wherever we ended up. I asked you to take me to a steakhouse, so you could order something bloody and disgusting."

He chuckled. "It's called rare meat, you moron."

She pretended to shudder. "Maybe you could distract me from the coming carnage with a rundown of your future aspirations."

He leaned forward on the table, bringing their faces closer. "I'd like to head up my own search and rescue team in a small town with endless miles of postcard pastures dotted with horses and cows."

"That's oddly specific." She leaned back in her seat to put more space between them.

"You wanna talk specifics?" His voice dropped to a husky tenor.

No, not really. She started to shake her head, but he kept talking.

"I'd eventually like to marry my best friend and maybe raise a couple of our own rascals together."

Her lips parted in surprise. Okay, that was way more than she'd bargained for when she brought up the topic of future aspirations. Apparently, it was going to take some shock and awe maneuvers to convince Lincoln she wasn't in the market for a boyfriend.

Lowering her gaze, she informed him softly. "Well, since we're baring our souls here, I might as well tell you that I got engaged to someone not too long ago, myself."

A stilted silence fell between them. "It's him, isn't it?" Lincoln's voice was stiff. "That soldier who went missing?"

"Yes." She drew a shaky breath. Although she

wasn't at liberty to tell her friend the full story, it was a relief to finally be honest about her reasons why the two of them couldn't date.

"Man! That's rough." He muttered something under his breath that she couldn't understand. "I knew you were keeping something from us. Clara said the same thing. No wonder you haven't been yourself lately."

The sympathy in his voice made her eyes mist.

"Does your dad know?"

She shook her head. "I didn't know how to tell him. It would've killed him to find out I've been waiting by the phone for a call that may never come."

He expelled a heavy breath. "So you're engaged to a soldier who's missing in action."

"I am."

"If I may ask, how long are you going to wait for him, Em?"

"As long as it takes to bring him home."

He sighed again. "Even if he's not...?"

"Alive?" She blinked rapidly, but a lone tear escaped and skidded down her cheek. "Yes. This one's worth waiting for, Linc."

"Okay. Man!" He reached for her hand. "Okay."

The rest of their meal passed in companionable silence, though he continued to pierce her with worried glances. Near the end, he finally spoke again. "Mind if I see your phone for a sec?"

"I already have your number."

"I know. I'm going to put it on speed dial." He made a come-hither motion. "Because that's what friends are for."

She mechanically reached inside the pocket of her hoodie, pulled out her phone, and handed it to him.

He opened it and stared curiously. "Is this a burner?"

Omigosh! "Yes." Her hand snapped out again, and she felt her face pale. "Don't ask questions."

"It's classified, huh?"

"Maybe. Just trade me, alright?" She dug for her personal cell and held it up.

Giving her a hard look, he made the exchange. "I won't ask questions, but I'll be adding Clara to your speed dial, as well." He punched in a few digits. "Hey, look! She's already in there. Maybe I'll add Owen, instead." He kept typing.

"You're a nut."

"Nuts about you."

She caught her lower lip between her teeth. "What part about I'm-already-engaged-to someone-else don't you understand?"

He shrugged. "Every team has back-up players, Em."

She half-rose from her seat to snatch her phone back. "I don't want you to put your life on hold for me."

"It's my choice to make."

"Then un-make it," she snapped.

"I will the moment you give me a reason to stop hoping." He glanced pointedly down at her hand.

Don't say it, please.

"Until I see a rock on your finger, I'm not giving up on us."

A-a-a-nd you said it. "That's it." She reached across the table. "Hand over your keys. You're so sleep-deprived that you don't know what's up or down."

She was a little surprised when he dropped his keys into her palm without putting up a fight. He curled her fingers over them. "This is me letting someone who cares look after me. You should try it sometime."

On a growl of irritation, she led the way back to his SUV. To her enormous relief, he dozed off and slept the rest of the way to her Dallas apartment. He didn't rouse until she put his vehicle in park and let the motor idle.

"Thanks." He stepped outside to unlatch the back door and drag out her suitcase. "I'll carry it up, if you want."

"That's okay, Officer Sleepyhead." She gave him a light shove. "Go home and catch some more Z's."

He grinned at her. "See? You do care about me."

She made a face. "Go."

He winked and hopped back inside his SUV. Waving, he drove away.

Shaking her head, she rolled her suitcase to the double glass doors of the three-story, red brick building. Scanning her membership badge, she let herself in and moved to stand before the elevators. Even though she'd slept well last night, she was feeling emotionally edgy from dealing with Lincoln's stubborn pursuit of her all afternoon.

Hopefully, Marcus would be on his way to Dallas soon. He'd promised to meet her here in a few days with a special license in hand, so they could get married. She was a thousand shades of excited about the new adventure they'd be embarking on together.

A few days ago, she'd been a single, very lonely Marine. And now she was about to marry the man of her dreams while starting a whole new and wonderful chapter of her career with the Marines — a chapter that actually involved working special ops. Talk about making it beyond the glass ceiling. *Shoot!* She was kicking the glass right out. It was almost too wow for words.

She rode the mirrored elevator car to the third floor and pushed her key inside the lock of the apartment at the far end of the hall. She was lucky to have rented an end unit on the top floor. Not only did she have a great view, it minimized the noise of apartment living.

Closing the door behind her, she paused to breathe in the solitude of home, and instantly grew still as the sound of a helicopter rumbled overhead.

Her burner phone pinged with an incoming message.

Change of plans. Just arrived. Need your authorization to enter the building.

What? She caught her breath. Marcus was already here? She hoped that didn't mean something had gone wrong.

Her call box buzzed with his request. Her fingers shook as she typed in her code. Seconds later, a knock sounded on her door.

As a precaution, she glanced through the keyhole. It was him. She threw open the door. "How did you—?"

He stepped inside, bolted the door behind him, and held out his arms.

She stepped into them.

"We flew a chopper here."

"We?"

"The colonel is with me. Sorry for the short notice. There's been a new development, which called for a detour here."

She hugged him fiercely. "Is everything okay?" He'd changed into distressed jeans and a black t-shirt that looked crazy good on him.

"I'm fine. Axel Hammerstone isn't. We just received word that someone attempted to vandalize his anesthesia line right before his latest surgery."

"How awful!"

"The colonel wants us down in San Antonio ASAP."

"Wow! You weren't kidding about the short notice." It didn't sound like there would be much time for goodbyes. Her father was going to be less than thrilled. They had a lunch date scheduled for Monday.

"When do we leave?"

"As soon as we get you packed, sweetheart."

She gazed around her tiny apartment. "Okay, then." She'd signed up for a position in covert operations. It sounded as if their adventures were beginning right away.

She started to step back, but Marcus's arms tightened around her. "Whoa there, beautiful! Aren't you forgetting something?"

The fast-paced insanity of the moment slowed when his lips touched hers. "Much better," he said softly, dragging his lips over hers a second time. "Sometimes it helps to be reminded of what we're fighting for."

She smiled against his lips. "Feel free to remind me as often as you wish."

"Yes, ma'am." He twirled her in her sneakers and dipped her low over his arm, making her feel like a princess.

"Nice moves." She touched his cheek when he tugged her upright once more.

He winked. "I have an extensive repertoire of

moves, babe."

She blushed, looking forward to experiencing each one. "Good. Start talking," she teased. "I want to know all about the man I'm going to marry, beginning with how long you've had your pilot's license."

"Still working on it. The colonel did most of the flying. I sat in as co-pilot."

She was familiar with his professional credentials, so she steered the conversation toward more personal topics next.

"Favorite color," she called merrily over her shoulder as she headed across the living room to her bedroom.

He followed her. "Red. Red apples. Red roses. Red cars. I own a red Corvette, by the way. Or did." He curled his lip. "I think Kiera's driving it these days. The little minx."

"Favorite kind of music," she called out next. Her bedroom had always been a cheerful hodgepodge of pinks and more pinks, but today it was in a special brand of shambles. She grimaced as they stepped over the threshold. She'd left in such a hurry, she hadn't taken the time to make her bed.

He gave a low whistle. "Looks like I am *not* marrying a neat freak."

"Hey! Don't judge me. Everything's clean, at least." She pulled open dresser drawers and rummaged around, making an even bigger mess.

He laughed at the spaghetti snarl in her sock

drawer. "When was the last time you matched your socks, beautiful?"

"Never." She slammed the drawer shut. "What's the point? All you need to do is put on two that mostly match, and..." Her voice grew muffled as she disappeared inside her closet.

He snickered. "How did you ever survive in the military?"

She popped her head out of the closet. "By relaxing the rules every night when I return home. And you never answered my question about music."

He grinned and assisted her in lifting down her suitcase from the top shelf. "I like listening to Christian, country, pop, a little rap now and then." He paused to lean against the door frame and watch her yank dresses and jackets off hangers. "My new favorite thing to listen to, though, is the sound of your voice."

Her face grew warm. "Good answer."

"I thought so." He folded his arms. "What about you? I can tell you like the color pink. What about your favorite music?"

"I like to sing."

"No kidding!"

"Yep. I was exploring the odds of landing a recording contract in Nashville before my last deployment."

"Seriously?"

"No, but I wish!" She chuckled merrily. "Maybe someday," she added wistfully.

"Sing something for me," he coaxed as she dashed past him to toss her half-full suitcase on the bed.

Flicking a self-conscious look his way, she hummed a few bars to find her key. Then she launched into an oldie but goodie, Amazing Grace.

To her delight, he joined in by the second line. Two important things were immediately apparent. Number one, he owned a powerful set of lungs to go along with his gorgeous baritone voice. Number two, he sang with such feeling that he had to be a man of faith. A third thing soon manifested itself — they made perfect harmony together.

THREE DAYS LATER, they learned a whole new melody and settled into a brand new rhythm when they exchanged their wedding vows. They met with a Marine chaplain on the rooftop of the San Antonio Military Medical Center.

Colonel Peterson stood in as their witness. His normally harsh features were graver than usual. "Because of the classified nature of your current positions, please understand that your real names cannot be officially recorded with the county registrar until after our mission is complete."

"Understood, sir." Marcus reached for her hands. "I'm sorry, sweetheart, but it's the only way to ensure that no one besides you figures out I'm still alive."

She nodded, thrilled that she was the one exception to the iron-clad rules he lived by as an undercover operative. The only shadow whatsoever on her happiness was that she wasn't able to share the joyful moment with her father or Marcus's family. *Some day,* she vowed. Some day they were going to renew their vows with both families present.

An early October wind whistled its way across the roofline, making Emma shiver in her blue-white dress uniform. They'd opted to remain in uniform for their ceremony, so as not to draw any extra attention to themselves. However, she'd substituted a white skirt for her slacks, and pumps in place of her low-quarter shoes. There was just no way she was getting married in trousers. *En oh spells no!*

It had been Marcus's idea to prepare their own vows. "I, Marcus Zane, take you, Emma Taylor, for my lawful wife, to have and to hold from this day forward as a reminder of everything we're fighting for — life, liberty, and the pursuit of happiness. I pledge all of me to all of you for better, for worse, for richer, for poorer, in sickness and health. I will love you and be faithful to you until my last breath."

Emma was moved to tears by the depth of her husband's promises. He was brave and loyal, a man who'd already proven he was willing to make great personal sacrifices to protect those he loved. She was humbled that he'd chosen to pledge his life to her.

She drew a shaky breath and plunged into her own vows. "I, Emma Taylor, take you, Marcus Zane, for my lawful husband, to have and to hold from this day forward. You complete all the missing pieces of me. Before I met you, I served because of duty and honor. Then you stepped into my world and added the miracle of love. You were worth waiting for when I had no real hope of ever seeing you again. And now that you've been mercifully returned to me, I am happy to pledge my life to you for better, for worse, for richer, for poorer, in sickness and health. I will love you forever and always."

Since they hadn't yet had the opportunity to shop for wedding rings, they exchanged black silicon bands that would be far more suitable for field work.

"After we successfully complete our mission, the first thing I'm going to do is replace this with a diamond." Marcus sealed his promise with a kiss.

They signed a temporary marriage certificate under the pseudonyms of Jane and Jack Smith, which would serve as their undercover names.

"Whelp!" After he scrawled his signature as their witness, Colonel Peterson surveyed them with satisfaction. "You're the first married couple who's ever served on one of my special teams, so this is going to be a new adventure for us all. My first official act as your handler is this." He produced a key.

"I hereby bestow on you the key to your castle. Or rather, to the safe house you'll be using as your base of operations in San Antonio."

"Thank you, sir." Ignoring protocol, Emma leaned in to give him a quick hug. "For everything." For being willing to take a chance on her, professionally. For serving as a witness and impromptu best man at their wedding. For opening the door to a whole new and exciting chapter of their lives.

The flush that rose to his swarthy features told her he appreciated the gesture. "My pleasure, sergeant." He hugged her back, showing a human side they didn't get to see very often. Normally he was all business, operating on one setting, only — emotional detachment.

Not for the first time, Emma wondered what the colonel's story was. Had he ever been married? Did he have children? Or any other family, for that matter? Unfortunately, none of their teammates had been made privy to his personnel file. It was one of those need-to-know things, and apparently Colonel Peterson didn't consider his personal life something any of them needed to know. She supposed it was a good thing he considered her and her new husband's lives a little more pertinent to the mission at hand.

Marcus shook their commander's hand and wasted no time in spiriting her away from the rooftop. However, he took an unexpected detour instead of heading straight to their safe house. Emma wrinkled her forehead as they approached a tall, stately city building. The sign indicated it belonged to the San Antonio Police Department.

"What are we doing here?" Did this mean Axel Hammerstone's saboteur had finally been identified and arrested?

"Collecting your wedding gift, sweetheart."

Oh. Wait, what? She couldn't have been more mystified. When had Marcus found the time to shop for gifts? Her heart sank a few degrees at the knowledge she had nothing to give him in return.

A sweet-faced young deputy led a dog out to them on a leash. He was a chocolate brown Labrador Retriever.

Emma's heart melted in understanding as the canine's wide, soulful eyes met hers. "Oh, you beautiful creature!" she breathed.

"His name is Goliath, and he's yours," Marcus announced proudly.

He couldn't have given her anything she would have treasured more. "My very own service dog." She felt like dancing with joy right there in the middle of the police department. "How can I ever thank you?"

His dark gaze glowed. "I'm sure you'll think of something, Mrs. Smith."

OVER THE NEXT SEVERAL WEEKS, Emma stuck to a rigorous schedule of guarding Axel Hammerstone and Hunt Ryker. So as not to interfere with their recovery, neither solder was informed that they were being targeted by a ruthless gang of arms dealers. Emma worked from the shadows, pulling endless patrols around the building perimeter, roof, and exterior grounds. Goliath quickly settled into serving as her faithful, and very protective, K9 partner.

Sadly, Marcus was called out of town two or three times per week to serve on sniper duty. Emma hated the necessity of being away from him so much, but she understood his services were in constant demand because he was the best at what he did.

They tried to make what few snatches of time they found together at the safe house really count. Unfortunately, the November election came and went without the big showdown with the corrupt senator that their team had worked so long and so hard to plan.

Colonel Peterson was livid. "I've never been so flabbergasted about anything in all my days," he spat. "I'm telling you, we're being sandbagged by our higher ups. No matter how much evidence I produce, they keep claiming our smoking guns aren't smoking hard enough."

Their mission quickly evolved into one of simply staying alive. Those on the team who were already presumed dead stepped up their efforts to protect the Marines lying in hospital beds with crosshairs on their foreheads. Their hope of receiving justice for the explosion in Kandahar grew fainter and fainter.

Their updated mission, however, wasn't the only new thing on the horizon. Emma woke with severe flu symptoms one morning. After a full medical exam, the medic delivered a mighty wallop.

"I'm pregnant?" she gasped, staring in horror at him. *No! I can't be. That so wasn't in the plan.* What was Marcus going to say? And how was this going to affect the rest of their team? Would Colonel Peterson fire her outright from his special task force?

CHAPTER 7: RUNNING

EMMA

Since Marcus was out of town on another sniper job, she wasn't able to share her news with him until the following evening.

To prepare him, she sent a few "drip" messages: *There's been a new development.*

She waited an hour before texting again: *We need to talk.*

The moment he walked into their safe house, he bolted the door and faced her grimly. "I know."

"What do you know?" She dragged her body from the faded plaid sofa in the living room where she'd wilted an hour earlier. She was so dizzy and nauseous she could hardly stand.

"Everything, beautiful. Now sit." He strode determinedly in her direction.

"I'm a soldier," she gritted out between clenched teeth. "I can stand on my own two blasted feet."

"Yeah? Well, you're a pregnant one." He bent to hook one steely arm under her knees and tenderly lifted her in his arms. He cuddled her against his chest and buried his face against her hair.

He wasn't angry. Tears of relief streamed down Emma's cheeks. They were followed by tears of weakness, tears of fear, and more tears for no reason at all.

In the end, he was the one who sat on the sofa with her securely ensconced in his lap.

"I'm so sorry," she muttered against his broad shoulder. *What are we going to do?*

He grew still. "Don't, Emma."

Her tears fell harder. "I know the timing is –"

"Don't be sorry for having my baby." He paused a beat. "Please."

She leaned back in his arms, surveying him in growing wonder. Despite the hopelessness of their situation, he seemed happy. "Our baby," she corrected with a sniffle.

He gave a low chuckle. "That's what I meant." He palmed her cheek and very gently drew her mouth to his.

For a moment, all her fears, all her pregnancy symptoms, and all the chaos outside the walls of their safe house disappeared.

He lifted his head a fraction to touch his forehead to hers. "I love you, Emma Zane. You're everything to me. That means protecting you and our unborn child is my new mission."

She gave a bleating gasp. "What do you mean?"

"Exactly what I said." He leaned back to draw a finger down her cheek. "As it stands, your obligation to the Marines ends today. Mine ends a week from now. I've already notified the colonel that I won't be reenlisting, and that I plan to throw all my efforts of persuasion into convincing you to do the same."

"You want us to leave the team?" she asked carefully.

"If that's what it takes to keep you safe."

"But I believe in what we're doing, Marcus. I don't want to quit."

"Good. I was hoping you'd say that." He gave her one of his slow, wicked smiles that made her heart dance crazily. "Who said anything about quitting?"

She twined her arms around his neck. If he could think of any way she could continue being useful while this sick and this pregnant, she was all ears. "So what's the plan?"

"I spent the last four hours negotiating a contract that will essentially allow us to continue doing what we're doing."

"Oh?" She traced a lazy circle on the back of his neck, reveling in his strength and nearness.

"As civilians."

"Still undercover, I presume?"

"Deep undercover this time. Still on salary. Still

working in conjunction with Colonel Peterson and his special task force. Still on mission, but from the civilian side of things. Kind of like CIA assets."

Emma drew a deep breath. "So you'll continue sniping, and I'll be doing what, exactly?"

He dipped his head to hold her gaze steadily. "Because of your MP experience, Colonel P says they could really use your help coordinating our mission from headquarters."

Her heart sank. "They're putting me on desk duty."

"It's temporary." Marcus splayed his hand across her still flat belly.

"Just call it what it is," she moaned. "I'm being completely sidelined."

"Actually, I don't see it that way at all." His expression was serious. "They're retaining you, because you're very good at what you do, officer."

"I guess."

"You guess?" He gave a bark of laughter.

"You're happy about this, aren't you, Daddy-O?" She poked his chest with a wry grimace.

"Maybe." He grinned. "I can't believe you're making such a big deal out of it. I mean, really. How many marathons do you feel like running right now, beautiful?"

She stuck her tongue out at him. "Hey, I could probably make it across the living room."

"Exactly." He drew her mouth back to his for

another very tender, very thorough kiss. Then he tucked her head against his shoulder. Running a hand through her hair, he spoke softly. "In the short time we've been together, I've asked a lot of you. I've asked you to stay strong for me. I've asked you to marry me. I've asked you to work undercover with me. And now I'm going to ask something else of you." His hand moved down her shoulder, all the way to her elbow, and made its way back to her belly. "Help me protect everything we have that's worth fighting for."

"You know I will." She inwardly shuddered at how difficult this next chapter was going to be. For the next seven or so months, at least.

"I can't do this without you, babe."

"Why, Marcus!" She straightened in his arms, not liking the bleakness of his voice. Then it hit her. He was happy about the baby, but he was terrified for her. For them. For their future. "You're never going to have to do this alone," she assured. "I promise."

He tipped his head back against the couch and gazed at her with his heart in his eyes. She'd never seen him this way. So raw. So vulnerable.

"Very glad to hear it." He reached out to touch her cheek. "I need your kisses and your sunshine. I need your messy sock drawer and the ridiculous amount of pink you've brought into my life." His dark eyes glinted with emotion. "I need you, Emma."

"You have me," she promised, cupping his face in her hands. "You have all of me. Forever and always."

This time they kept their eyes open when they kissed, drinking each other in, memorizing the love they read in each other's eyes.

THEY WOULD REMEMBER that moment for the next several months when their lives became exponentially difficult. They would treasure it and draw strength from it. And they would live in the hope of some day enjoying another such moment.

Emma's pregnancy quickly turned hellish. She grew so sick that she was finally hospitalized. Well, a covert form of being hospitalized, anyway. She was placed in a hospital bed in their safe house on complete bedrest beneath the watchful eye of an undercover nurse.

To make matters worse, she went into labor two and a half weeks early while Marcus was out of town. Knowing there was no way he would make it in time, she sent him an emergency text on the burner phone.

We're having the baby today.

Even if he couldn't be there, he deserved to know. Through streaming tears, she broke protocol and sent him play-by-play updates.

Eight centimeters dilated. This is happening!

To her alarm, Marcus neither called nor responded to her messages. In the end, Goliath was the only family member present when their baby made his first appearance into the world. The dog stuck like a cocklebur to her side, even when the midwife tried to shoo him away. He stubbornly laid his snout on her shoulder and remained there until her infant son's cries filled the bedroom of the safe house.

Once the midwife bathed the baby and helped Emma clean up, she sent a final text to her husband with a heavy heart. His continued silence worried her that something was terribly wrong.

Our mocha baby is here! How do you like the name Jackson? After your grandfather...

She gazed down at the tiny, six and a half pound, fist-waving miracle in her arms. He was on the small side since he was born a bit early, but he was perfect. She nuzzled his silky dark head of hair and porcelain cheeks with a murmur, "You're going to completely lasso your daddy's heart the moment he sees you."

She glanced up as the midwife finished packing her bag. *Where are you, Marcus?* It was unlike him to be unresponsive for this long, especially at a time like this. He'd known when he left town how close she was to her delivery date.

Sadly, her only visitor in the next few hours was Colonel Peterson. "I'm sorry, Emma." His expression was drawn, and he looked ten years older than when she'd last seen him.

"Tell me what's going on, sir." She sat up with a wince, knowing he would have the answers she was seeking about her husband. "No more new mama coddling." She felt battered and sore, but she was no longer pregnant. Her body would only get stronger from this point on. "Where is he? I can handle the truth."

He gingerly took a seat on the edge of her mattress. "Mind if I hold him?" His heavily scarred hands reached for Jackson.

"Of course." With a smile, she transferred the tiny bundle to him. His harsh expression gentled as he gazed at her son. It was like finally getting a glimpse at that heart of gold Marcus had always insisted the man had.

He expertly cradled the babe against his black cargo jacket, telling her it wasn't the first time he'd held an infant. "They've put out a hit on your husband. That's why you haven't heard from him. He's being forced to lie low."

She immediately knew he was talking about the arms dealers. "Who leaked his name?" Her heart pounded with dread. All through her pregnancy, this had been one of her worst fears.

The colonel scowled down at Jackson, who was sleeping soundly. "We don't have any reason to believe they've uncovered his true identity."

"Yet," she snapped.

"Yet," he agreed heavily. "All they know is he's a sniper. One who's caused a serious amount of trouble for them. They blame his interference for the delay of their last two arms shipments. They're also crediting him for taking out three key terrorists."

"Do they know he's a Marine?"

The colonel raised his hard, silvery gaze to hers. "If they don't, they have their suspicions. His style of work has military training written all over it."

She shook her head, feeling defeated. "You know what? I'm tired, colonel." She appreciated the fact that he didn't immediately shoot back with some nonsense about her exhaustion having to do with being a new mother. It was more than that. She was tired to her very soul. Tired of fighting battles it was starting to feel like they would never win.

"I'm tired, too, sergeant." His voice was strangely bitter.

"Tell me, colonel. Why are we still fighting?" She knew the answer, but she wanted to hear his take on it. As she waited, she picked at a thread on the blanket covering her knees. More than anything, she was tired of this shabby house with its peeling paint. She was sick of lying in bed. And she was insanely fed up with the color white. She wanted some pink back in her life. Any shade of it. Fuchsia, salmon, mauve... Just bring it on already!

When he didn't answer right away, she

continued grumbling. "Some days I can hardly tell the good guys from the bad guys." Their higher ups continually handed down missions, while those in office strapped so much red tape on them that it was next to impossible to do their jobs. Most notably, there were arms traffickers still at large who were likely getting assistance from the inside — traffickers who were more determined than ever to disappear the entire Marine unit who'd dared to get in their way.

"You're the good guys, Sergeant Zane," Colonel Peterson droned in a low rumble. "You and every Marine who ever put their life on the line to fight this nation's battles, and I'm going to make sure the good guys win if it's the last thing I do." He handed Jackson back and leaned over to smooth a hand over his dark hair. "The future of this little fella depends on the good guys winning."

"How can I help?" Emma asked softly, tucking her son's blanket more securely around his sleeping form.

"By sitting this one out."

Story of my life. "How is that going to help?" She was aghast. It was one thing to be sidelined because she was pregnant. It was another thing, entirely, to keep her there after the fact.

"You don't want to give the arms dealers any extra ammunition to fire at your husband right now."

"Meaning me and Jackson," she supplied dully.

"Yes. You're already a target because of your connection to the Marines in Kandahar, but God forbid your connection to your sniper husband is ever made known to them."

"What are you suggesting?"

"You need to keep a low profile, Emma. As in go completely off the grid, so they can never use you as bait to drag your husband out of hiding." He held out a hand, palm up. "That includes giving up your burner phone."

She recoiled against the pillows. "But it's my only connection to him." It was their one full-proof line of communication when it wasn't safe to get in touch any other way. She fisted her hand around the phone in her pocket, unable to bring herself to relinquish it.

"That's why you need to sever it — for his safety and yours." The colonel sighed at her expression. "There's no point in putting up a fight, Emma. I already collected your husband's burner."

How dare you! Waves of helpless rage washed over her as she stared at her boss. She understood military service and patriotic missions. She knew her duty. But this? This was crossing a line. Her lips trembled. "If this is about those messages I sent him while I was in labor..."

Colonel Peterson's split-second hesitation, along with the faint ripple of puzzlement across his brow, raised every warning flag inside her. He didn't appear to be familiar with her frantic, in-labor updates, which meant he wasn't actually in possession of Marcus's burner phone. At least not yet. He was lying.

In the next moment, his normally stoic features stretched into a ferocious glare. "That's exactly what I'm talking about! So unless you want the arms dealers to find out about Jackson, you're just going to have to trust me on this, Emma Dil." He reached for her phone again.

Emma Dil? She blinked at the strange light in his eyes, truly unnerved by now. *Who is Emma Dil?* As her mind raced over her options, she desperately latched on to one — to get one final message to Marcus before going on radio silence.

"Fine!" she snarled, pretending to fume. "You're right, sir, and I hate it that you're right."

The stiffness in his shoulders relaxed.

"And since I happen to be an angry, hormonal new mother at the moment, you're going to have to stand there and watch me send one last message to no one."

"Emma!" he warned, beckoning again for her to pass over the phone.

Great, I'm back to being just plain ol' Emma again. She scowled at him. "I'll read it out loud while I type to save you the trouble of having to snoop through my messages later."

To her relief, he bought into the fiction she was

spinning and waited. He shifted from one boot to the other, his irritation broiling to a nearly palpable level.

"Dearest Marcus," she cooed, shooting the colonel what she hoped was a teasing look. "Actually, I haven't started typing yet." Was he really a colonel? Or was he some two-bit imposter? She held up the phone and punched in a few letters. "Gonna pay a visit to my sisters." That was it. That was the whole message. She pushed send. Marcus would know something was amiss when he read it — *if* he was still in possession of his burner phone, which she suspected he was.

"You don't have any sisters," Colonel Peterson noted suspiciously.

"True," she retorted cheerfully, tossing the phone his way at last.

He caught it with one hand, without removing his gaze from hers.

"It's a private joke. Every time Marcus and I do undercover work in public, I always jabber about my imaginary, shopaholic sisters. You should see the number of head nods we get. It's something nearly everyone can relate to."

The colonel smiled without mirth. "I once had a wife who liked to shop."

A wife named Emma Dil, maybe? Emma gave a small murmur of sympathy. "I couldn't help wondering if you have a family."

"Had." His expression hardened. "Past tense."

She wondered what happened, but he didn't volunteer any more information. Instead, he slapped a roll of dollar bills on her mattress. It was the biggest wad of cash she'd ever laid eyes on in her life.

"What's this?"

"Exactly what it looks like. I want you to use it to go off grid and stay off grid."

Her eyes widened. "For how long?"

"For as long as you want to stay alive," he growled. His eyes glinted like silver fire. "Your husband should've never brought you on board in the first place." After that strangely insulting shot, he stomped from the bedroom. She heard him traverse the living area. Then the front door clicked shut behind him.

She stared after him, thoroughly shaken at what had just transpired. So he wanted her to go on the run, did he? He wanted her to sideline herself so he didn't have the added guilt of harming a woman and a baby on top of whatever heinous activities he was up to his eyeballs in.

She gingerly threw her legs over the side of her hospital bed and sat there with her head bowed over Jackson. It was no wonder their special task force had experienced one setback after another while attempting to stop the arms traffickers. Not only was Colonel Peterson in cahoots with the arms dealers, he was additionally running the investigative team assigned to bring them to justice. No doubt he'd been running interference in the investigation since day one. What an absolute scumbag!

Well, if he thought he could sideline her just because she was a new mother, he was sorely mistaken. She didn't mind making it look like she'd gone on the run. She didn't mind letting him think he'd bested in the short-term, but she had every intention of doing the opposite. She'd promised her husband he would never have to fight this fight alone, and she'd meant every word of it.

With a groan, she forced herself to her feet. Gosh, but she felt about as energetic as roadkill. Giving birth to a baby was no joke. She gently rocked Jackson, trying to get her sea legs as she pondered what to do next. After months of working under-cover, she'd learned a thing or two about hiding in plain sight. The more she thought about it, the more she liked the idea of not going very far when she went off the grid. Plus, staying close would give her a little more time to get back on her feet before taking the fight back to Peterson and his cronies.

After her mind was made up, she packed as many supplies as she could fit in a single backpack — the cash, her personal IDs, and as many baby diapers and blankets as she could fit around her military gear.

Then she whistled for Goliath. "Come on, boy. We have a bus to catch." This she said for the benefit of anyone who might be listening. It was wise at this juncture to assume the safe house had been bugged.

Her service dog gave a low growl of acquiescence and trotted her way to accept his harness and leash. Since the colonel was probably expecting her to convalesce a day or two, it was best for them to leave now.

Emma walked to the nearest Goodwill store a few blocks down the street, purchased a different outfit, and searched for the restroom sign. Fortunately, it was a small store with a solo bathroom, so she was able to lock herself in. After changing, she took a few minutes to nurse Jackson. Then she guzzled down the first of her two water bottles.

Next stop was the bus station. Sort of... She had a baby and a dog to hide first — after she ditched her cell phone, that is. Unfortunately, the men she was running from would be able to use it to track her whereabouts. Sighing, she whipped out her phone and painstakingly wrote down the most important numbers in her address book. Then, with a wince of misery, she dropped the device on the floor and ground it beneath her boot.

Keeping her head down, she exited the restroom and cut through the *Employees Only* warehouse in the back to reach the rear exit.

"Ma'am, you can't be in here," a man's voice warned.

She gave an offhand wave without looking up. "Sorry. I made a wrong turn out of the bathroom. I'm leaving right now." She made a beeline for the loading dock and hurried down the stairs. Hopefully, the maneuver would make her a little harder to follow.

Keeping to the alley, she skirted the back of several more plaza stores in search of a pay phone. She found one at the edge of a pothole-ridden parking lot. Popping in a few coins, she dialed Lincoln. He was going to give her an earful the next time he saw her, but she didn't have many options right now.

"Officer Hudson speaking." His voice was crisp and not overly inviting.

"Linc," she breathed, wildly grateful that he'd picked up. The odds were like a thousand to one.

"Emma!" His voice sharpened with recognition. "I don't recognize this number. Did you get a new cell phone?"

"It's a payphone."

"Oka-a-a-y. Mind telling me where you've been? Or is that a state secret?"

She kept her voice low. "It's a long story."

"Really? Well, I've got plenty of time, so—"

"I don't," she cut in. "Listen, how far of a drive

are you from..." She rattled off the location of the hair salon on the other side of the parking lot.

"How did you know I was in the area?" he demanded suspiciously.

"You're in town?" She gave an involuntary squeal of exultation, then immediately clapped a hand over her mouth. "How soon can you get here?"

"Listen, are you in some sort of trouble?" The suspicion in his voice was replaced with worry.

"Yes." *You have no idea.*

"And you called me." He sounded supremely satisfied with that fact.

"Linc," she warned.

"I'm on my way." He disconnected the line.

In less than ten minutes, he nosed his navy SUV into the parking lot. She waited until he circled in her direction before stepping out of the shadows and waving.

He jammed on his brakes and leaped from the vehicle. Before he could yell her name, she pressed a finger to her lips.

He glanced around them, a scowl painted across his angular features. "Here." He flung open one of the side doors.

Grateful for the tinted windows, she winced as she climbed inside and whistled for Goliath to follow her.

Shaking his blonde head at her, Lincoln leaped behind the wheel and slammed his door shut.

The sharp noise woke Jackson and made him whimper.

"What the—?" Lincoln met Emma's gaze in alarm through his rearview mirror.

"Please," she whispered. "Just drive to the bus station."

He drove. "You know there's nothing I wouldn't do for you, Emma Taylor. But, so help me God, you better start talking."

She nodded. There was something about being in the safety of a friend's vehicle that twanged every nerve, bringing her tangle of emotions to the surface. "I found him, Linc. He's alive."

Lincoln drew a heavy breath. "The missing soldier you claimed to be in love with?"

"Yes. I married him."

"And?" His gaze clashed with hers in the mirror. "It's like you dropped off the face of the earth months ago, Emma."

"I took an undercover job with him."

"Undercover, huh?" His voice was rough. "I take it, the baby is yours?"

She nodded tearfully. "This is Jackson."

"I don't even know what to say."

"How about congratulations?"

"Seriously?" he snarled, glancing over his shoulder to get a better look at her. "You actually expect me to congratulate you for marrying a ghost who's left you on the run with a new baby?"

"We were double-crossed, and they put a hit on my husband's head. It's not his fault."

Lincoln clenched his jaw. "So what's the plan? I help you leave town, and you disappear for good this time?"

Maybe. I don't know. "Actually, I only need you to help me make it look like I left town. I plan to stick around and see this thing through."

"This thing," he repeated coolly.

"That's all I can tell you." She dug in her backpack and unearthed her driver's license along with the wad of money Colonel Peterson had given her. "I need you to go inside the bus station and purchase at least a dozen one-way tickets with this. Make sure they're going in all different directions. Then I need you to plant the tickets around the waiting area, so other people will find them and use them."

"Whatever, Emma," he sighed, pulling into the parking lot of the bus station. It was growing dark. He grabbed a curb spot beneath a streetlight. Switching off the ignition, he twisted around in his seat to hand her the key. "Just in case you need to make a quick getaway, Hollywood."

She smiled gratefully. "I owe you big-time."

"Yeah, you do."

He snatched up the money and her ID and yanked open his door. While Lincoln was gone, she nursed Jackson again. By the time he returned, she was sagging with exhaustion against the plush leather seat back.

Lincoln slid behind the wheel and sat there in silence for several moments. "Exactly how old is your baby, Emma?"

"I had him today." Her voice sounded as thin and as brittle as she felt.

"That's it." He motioned for her to return his keys. "I'm taking you to the hospital."

"No, Linc! You can't!" She fisted his keys in the air. "Not if you ever want to see me alive again."

"Emma!" he groaned.

She swallowed hard. "What I need is a place to disappear for a while. Some place outside the city but not too far outside. There are two Marines in the hospital I've been guarding."

Lincoln gave a snort of disbelief. "Who's guarding you and Jackson?"

She reached over to pat the head of her service dog. "Goliath."

He pointed at his keys she was still brandishing. "May I?"

She tossed them.

He caught them and started his engine. "There's a woman who lives in Glen Rose, who's like a grandmother to me. If I ask her, she'll give you a place to crash."

"Is she the reason you're in town?" Emma knew it was hardly fair of her to keep prying for information about him, when she wasn't in the position to tell him much about her own situation.

"Yes."

She leaned her head back against the seat again, feeling lightheaded. "You're a good man, Lincoln."

"And don't you forget it," he returned. There was a hint of humor in his voice this time.

"Any chance we can pick up a bag of dog food and some diapers on the way there?" she sighed.

"Yep. Probably wouldn't hurt to snag a carseat, too," he noted dryly, eyeing the sleeping infant in her arms.

"Good idea," she mumbled and started to drift.

The next thing she knew, Lincoln was jostling her shoulder and Goliath was growling out a protest.

"It's okay, boy." She smiled wryly at Lincoln. "I'm a horrible dog mommy. Poor thing hasn't eaten since this morning."

A grandmotherly face peeked around the open door. "Oh, Lincoln! You said a baby. You didn't say a brand spanking new one." The woman eagerly extended her plump arms.

Emma mustered a tired smile as she handed him over. "Thank you for letting us stay with you. I'm Jane Smith, by the way."

"Nice to meet you, Jane." The woman winked at her as if they shared a particularly juicy secret. "I'm Melba. Melba Hayes. And this grandma is very happy to have visitors." She headed inside with Jackson cradled in her arms.

Lincoln watched her disappear inside her one-story cottage before turning back to Emma.

She winced as she scooted across the seat to get out.

"You okay?" he asked quickly.

"If by okay, you mean feeling like I was run over by a train," she whimpered. "Then, yes. I'm peachy."

"So will your ghost of a husband shoot me if I carry you inside?"

"Probably...," she teased, "not."

"Good, because I wasn't planning on asking for permission." He gently lifted her from the back seat.

She gratefully sagged against him, thankful all over again that he'd picked up when she'd called.

TO BOTH HER relief and dismay, Lincoln lingered in Glen Rose for another three days to help her get settled. And despite her efforts to protect him by keeping him out of her personal business, he managed to wrangle enough information out of her about the injured Marines to be of some real help to them. He called in a few favors and managed to get a retired police officer friend embedded as a Red Cross volunteer on their ward. More eyeballs on the scene meant more protection for Axel and Hunt. It also made it possible for Emma to remain solidly off the grid.

To avoid being a complete burden on Melba, she applied for a job at a local diner. From a Marine, to a special forces operative, to a waitress who was secretly married to a ghost, her life sure hadn't gotten any simpler.

CHAPTER 8: FINAL DESCENT

MARCUS

It had been two months since Marcus had last heard from Emma. He was insane with worry as he read her last text message for the thousandth time.

Gonna pay a visit to my sisters. Since she had no sisters, he'd taken the message for what it was — a warning. All he could fathom was that her position had been compromised the day she'd delivered Jackson — a day he'd most unfortunately been forced into hours of radio silence on the colonel's orders. Afterward, his wife and son had vanished into thin air.

Colonel Peterson was less helpful than Marcus anticipated. He initially helped retrace Emma's steps to the bus station, but there the trail ran cold. Thirteen tickets had been purchased in her name, and seven of them had been used. She'd rather masterfully covered her tracks. It told him two things: She was alive, and she had deliberately gone off the grid. But why? And why had she done it without leaving him a way to contact her?

She wouldn't have. Plain and simple. And that was what had him the most worried. Something — or someone — must have forced her hand and left her with no choice but to go into hiding.

I'm going to find you, sweetheart. It was the first vow he made every morning when he awoke and the last prayer on his lips each night when he tumbled atop his bedroll.

Several more weeks passed before he ran across the first clue concerning his wife's whereabouts. It was one of those completely-by-accident, totally-random types of things. And it was bad...

Since Emma was no longer at her usual post, Colonel Peterson was flying them to San Antonio to oversee Hunt Ryker's final exit from the military post. It had been a full fourteen months since that fateful explosion in Kandahar. Fourteen months of surgeries and therapy sessions. Word on the grapevine had it that his unit was planning a special awards ceremony for him on his way out. They were going to pin on a Purple Heart.

Marcus longed to congratulate his friend, but his status as an undercover operative wouldn't allow any personal contact. Like a ghost, he was going to have to witness Hunt's awards ceremony from the shadows. He ran a hand over his shaved head. As of late, he was getting deathly tired of living in the shadows. Their undercover mission, which had started off as a patriotic and worthwhile protective detail, was waning into an exhaustive tangle of corruption that threatened to drag on forever.

Every night, Marcus dreamed of the day when he would get his life back. He longed for the day he could introduce his wife and son to his parents and sister. Right now, though, he'd settle for meeting his son for the first time. Everything else on his wishlist could come after that.

Yanking out his burner phone, he shot off another hopeless message to Emma, not expecting to hear anything back. If she was wise — and she was — she'd probably long since trashed both of her phones.

Hope you and Jackson are okay. Miss you like crazy. He pushed send.

There was a small vibration against his left boot. Glancing down, he noted the colonel's backpack had slid across the floor and was now resting against his ankle. He nudged it away with his toe.

The colonel eyed the burner phone in Marcus's hands. "Still no answer?"

Marcus shook his head. "Nope. I'm afraid she's completely in the wind."

The colonel's answering smirk made little sense. He reached up to adjust his headset. They were speaking to each other through their mouthpieces. "She's a real firecracker, that wife of yours."

"Yeah." Loneliness slammed into Marcus. What he wouldn't give to hear her voice again! He could barely stand the sight of anything pink these days.

"She's okay wherever she is. You know that, right?" His team leader angled his head questioningly.

"I'd like to think that, sir." Marcus's voice cracked. He cleared his throat and lapsed into silence.

"So this friend of yours, Hunt Ryker."

"Uh-huh." Marcus was barely listening. He was too busy typing another message to his wife.

"Thought you might want to know he's been poking around for information about you." The colonel banked right for a turn as he positioned himself for their landing. His backpack slid across the floor again.

I love you, sweetheart. Marcus pushed send. Like before, there was an answering vibration against his boot.

His gaze snapped to the colonel's backpack. *What the—?* To test his suspicions, he zinged off another three text messages. Each time, there was an answering vibration against his boot, telling him that his wife's burner phone was in Colonel Peterson's backpack.

You've got to be kidding me! Marcus's hand inched toward his pistol. He waited until the colonel was looking the other way before whipping it out and pressing it to his temple.

"Where is she?"

His team leader didn't so much as twitch an eyelash. If anything, he grinned. "You got something on your mind, son?"

"I know you have her phone."

"Took you long enough to figure it out."

"Where. Is. She?" Marcus repeated icily.

"In the wind like you said, son."

"Quit calling me that!"

The colonel's upper lip curled. "All I can tell you is, I gave her a load of money and sent her off the grid, thereby freeing you up to do your job." His demeanor was as nonchalant as a chess player moving a pawn across a game board.

"Are you out of your mind?" Marcus cried. *This is my wife we're talking about!* The colonel's betrayal stabbed through him like a thousand knives.

"It's about the mission, son. It's always been about the mission." Colonel Peterson's glance was laced with pity. "And sometimes sacrifices must be made. You should've never gotten your sweet wife mixed up in this."

"Sacrifices!" Marcus gaped at him. "What do you know about sacrifices?" Between the two of them, he was the one who'd given up the most for their mission. Well, he and Digby MacLamore, anyway.

"Quite a lot, actually." The colonel shoved away the butt of Marcus's pistol. "You may as well put that thing away. We both know you'd never shoot an unarmed man." He made a sound of derision. "Even if you wanted to." He shook his head. "There are some lines you choir boys will never cross. Which, incidentally, is what made you such a valuable member of the team."

Made. Past tense. "Name one sacrifice you've made," Marcus snarled. "Just one." Now that they were discussing it, the colonel had always been content to sit back and let the rest of his soldiers do the heavy lifting.

"Kandahar wasn't my first explosion, son. The one in Kabul a few years ago took out my wife. Her name was Emma Del, in case anybody cares." He made a face as if tasting something sour. "Then there were the explosions in Zabul and along the Tarnak River. And don't get me started on the endless firestorms in Pakistan. For soldiers who consider themselves to be members of a peacekeeping force, we sure leave a long trail of civilian casualties everywhere we go, eh?"

They were hovering over the San Antonio River by now. Marcus stared at his team leader in disbelief. "So this was never about protecting the Marines. This was about..." He shook his head in disgust.

"Go ahead and say it, son," Colonel Peterson ordered with a mad-sounding chuckle.

Horror tightened Marcus's chest. The man was completely off his rocker.

"If you won't say it, I will. Our secret mission was to neutralize the United States Marines and every other weapons-wielding nation before they could hurt anyone else."

What secret mission? "So you're saying the whole mission was garbage from the get-go?" Or there never really was a mission to begin with. Marcus felt his temper escalating to explosive levels. "Does this mean that the Marines whose lives we're watchdogging were never even being targeted?"

"I wouldn't say that." Peterson shrugged. "It only made sense to keep tabs on the soldiers who might've seen something incriminating. Fortunately, most of them have proven not to be a threat. Well, mostly. Hunt Ryker might become a problem if he does much more poking around."

Marcus couldn't believe what he was hearing. "You were like a father to me. I trusted you." *Boy, did you have me fooled!* He said this more to himself than the madman sitting across from him.

Colonel Peterson grimaced as the chopper began its final descent. "And you were like a very useful son." He paused a beat. "Until you weren't."

"Now I'm just one more loose end to tie up, eh?"

"Something like that. I'm sorry it has to be this way. It's not personal. You're a great soldier, but I have arms dealers demanding someone's head on a platter, and yours just happens to be the one they want the most." He peered out the window. "I know you're probably fantasizing about putting a bullet through me or crashing the 'copter, so let me help you out with that decision. There are men on the ground waiting to take you into custody. If you go peacefully, you'll be leaving a lovely widow and a happy and whole infant son behind." He offered a bleak smile. "If you don't go peacefully, well, let's just say there will be a manhunt underway shortly for your terrorist partner, Emma Taylor."

Marcus gave a huff of disbelief. He'd heard enough. "I choose option three." In a flash, he reared back his leg and kicked the corrupt colonel straight from the open-sided cockpit. The last thing he saw was the man's shocked, open-mouthed expression as he plummeted toward the river.

The chopper teetered precariously as Marcus slid behind the controls. He swiftly took over and righted the craft. Then he ascended into the sky and set his course for their team's latest base of operations.

If only he could reach them before any of Peterson's cronies did! Well, he'd find out soon enough if he succeeded. They'd either welcome him as a returning comrade or come charging at him guns-a-blazing.

It took a little over an hour to reach the weathered shack. Located in a remote field adjacent to the grounds of the Texas Hotline Training Center, it looked abandoned from its half-hidden crouch in the trees. However, Marcus knew that operations were very much alive behind its soundproof walls.

Dig MacLamore could attest to it. He'd been embedded there for weeks, watchdogging over their friend, Hunt Ryker, who'd accepted an instructor role at the training center.

As the chopper rumbled through its descent, Dig stepped from a side door and shaded his eyes to watch. A pair of federal agents joined him. Even from his bird's-eye-view, Marcus could tell they were CIA from their predictable dark suits and tinted sunglasses.

He cut the motor and dashed half-bent beneath the whirring blades.

Dig strode in his direction, grinning. "How ya?" he drawled, lapsing into his thick native brogue. Then he leaned in to slap Marcus on the back. He followed up the slap with a full Irish buss on the cheek.

"I'm alive," Marcus muttered.

The irony of his words weren't missed by Dig. "Where's the colonel?" he asked quickly, glancing around his friend's shoulder.

"At the bottom of the San Antonio River, unless he's a really good swimmer." By his best estimate, he'd dropped the guy a good fifty to seventy-five feet above the water.

"Ah. You discovered his duplicity."

Marcus shook his head, still reeling with disbelief. "In the nick of time, my friend." In the very narrowest nick.

The helicopter was soon crawling with intelligence agents. They canvased every inch of the craft and stripped it down to its floorboards. Marcus watched through narrowed eyes as they removed Colonel Peterson's backpack, all the chopper's electronic equipment, even the upholstered seats.

HE AND DIG were detained an additional forty-eight hours for questioning and debriefing. Apparently, the crusty old Colonel Peterson had survived his tumble into the river. Due to a breakthrough in the money trail investigation only hours earlier, however, there were federal agents waiting at the water's edge to take him into custody. He was expected to face a military tribunal on multiple charges of war crimes.

In the meantime, Marcus and Dig found it hard to complain about the delay in their return to Dallas, since the CIA transported them to a five-star hotel and allowed them to bathe and eat. They were even given suits to change into, which both of them found mildly humorous. Neither could remember the last time they'd worn anything fancier than cargo pants or board shorts.

Though mindlessly exhausted, however, both of them refused to sleep until the agency contacted their wives. They reached Jillian MacLamore first.

Dig broke down and wept openly when her tearfully joyful face appeared on the big screen the agents had erected in a private meeting room. By Marcus's best estimate, the two of them hadn't laid eyes on each other in nearly fifteen months. The big Irishman unashamedly reached out to splay his hand against the screen when their son held out his arms. JT had been born while Dig was deployed. He was over a year old now — a walking, talking bundle of little boy energy.

Wondering what his own son looked like, Marcus quietly exited the room to give the MacLamore family their privacy. Weariness slammed into him the moment the door shut behind him. He paced the private lounge attached to their suite. *Please, God, keep my wife and son safe. Bring them home to me.*

His vision blurred as he prayed. Some might have scoffed at his current actions, but begging for miracles was truly the last trick he had left in his bag. Thanks to the colonel, all means of communication with Emma had been stripped away. Though the CIA had promised to search for her, he knew it was like digging for a needle in the proverbial haystack.

As much as it was breaking his heart to be apart from her like this, however, he was proud at how thoroughly she'd taken herself and their son off the grid. She was highly trained and far tougher than she looked. She was a survivor. He didn't doubt for a second that their son was safe in her care.

As the sun dipped below the horizon, a knock sounded on the door. Assuming it was yet another agent interrupting his solitude for yet another round of questioning, he took his time crossing the room.

As expected, a suited-up agent was standing on the other side. "Well, Mr. Zane," the man looked sheepish, "I'm sorry to say we didn't find your wife, but," his expression brightened, "I'm very happy to report that she *did* find us."

After that astonishing announcement, he stepped aside. And there she was.

"Emma!" Marcus cried hoarsely. *Sweetheart!*

She looked like an angel, standing in the doorway in a white sundress. Her blonde hair was longer than he remembered, cascading like a silk waterfall over her honey-tan shoulders.

After a moment of stunned silence, she half-sobbed and half-shrieked his name. "Marcus!" Then she flew across the threshold into his outstretched arms.

He caught her and spun her in a full circle. The earth seemed to tilt, and heaven seemed to touch down as their lips found each other. He tasted her frantic joy and unwavering adoration, and was lost in the wonder of knowing that he was still hers and she was still his.

A faint whimper finally tore through the magic, bringing his head from the clouds. "Jackson," he whispered in awe, setting his wife back on her feet. He turned with her in his arms to face the glorious sound.

A stroller he hadn't noticed before was resting just beyond the doorway. A tall, chocolate Labrador Retriever was sitting proudly next to it.

"I've been dying to introduce the two of you!" Emma tugged at her husband's arm and led him across the room to their squirming, dark-haired infant.

"My son." Marcus reached out blindly, and she lifted the precious bundle into his arms.

CHAPTER 9: HOMECOMING

EMMA

The strains of organ music wafted through the rafters of the old church cathedral in Dallas. Emma stared down at her white silk wedding gown, hardly able to believe she was finally getting to be the bride.

Well, technically, she'd officially become a bride ten months earlier, but their families had pooh-poohed the notion of doing a mere vow renewal ceremony. Instead, they'd put their heads together and planned a big church wedding with hundreds of friends, a towering cake, and all the hoopla.

Clara's laughing, pixie-like features appeared in the mirror beside hers. They were standing in an old prayer room adjacent to the foyer. A prism of sunlight from a tall, stained glass window was making a rainbow of colors dance across her face. "Was it just a few days ago, you were bemoaning the fact that you were always a bridesmaid and never a bride?"

Emma blinked back happy tears and shook her head. "Days, months...but who's counting?" She had Marcus to thank for rescuing her from a life of endless bridesmaid dresses.

"I think you were, darling." Clara's blue eyes sparkled. "And after meeting the hunky Marine you've been hiding from us all this time, I can guarantee you he was counting the days, as well. Your love story is total movie material. The two of you should write a book about it someday."

"He is pretty amazing, isn't he?"

"If that's what they're calling drop-dead gorgeous real American heroes these days? Then, yes." Her friend's expression changed suddenly, and her pink petal lips pursed in speculation. "I'm still trying to wrap my poor brain around the fact that the two of you were enjoying a major smooch-fest out there in the sand dunes on the night of my wedding!"

Emma blushed.

"After I'd spent a good amount of the weekend trying to set you up with my own stepbrother."

Emma's blush deepened. "Even though things didn't work out between Lincoln and me, he's still the best." Rock solid and pure gold. She was fortunate to count a man of his caliber as her friend.

"He says the same about you." Clara made a face. "If only you had a twin sister," she sighed.

Emma shared her friend's distress on Lincoln's behalf. He was such a wonderful guy. He deserved to have an equally wonderful woman in his life.

The sound of a man clearing his throat had them spinning around. The sight of their newest visitor made all worries about Lincoln's love life disappear.

"Dad!" Emma glided in his direction.

A man of medium height, he bent to kiss her cheek, brushing her jaw with his frosted blonde goatee. "Something tells me your mother is looking down on us from above today." He dug in his pocket and unearthed a gold locket. Opening it, he displayed a cameo of her. "But this will guarantee her a front row seat." He leaned down to clasp the thin gold chain around his daughter's neck.

"I love it." She drenched him with a happy smile. "Thank you." There was nothing she wished more than to have her mother's memory close to her heart during their upcoming promenade down the aisle.

"My pleasure, Mrs. Zane. Shall we?" He crooked his arm at her and led her to the wide, arched doorway leading into the sanctuary. The last bridesmaid was nearly finished sashaying her way to the altar.

Next, a stringed quartet struck the opening notes of the wedding march. The church organist chimed in, and Emma floated down the aisle on her father's arm.

Hundreds of her and Marcus's friends and

family were packed inside the pews. People she'd gone to high school with, countless Marines, and several clusters of men and women in suits that she suspected were federal agents. She was pretty sure she recognized another style of uniform in the crowd, too — the solid black outfits worn by the cadre at the Texas Hotline Training Center. According to Axel and Hunt, the leadership there was very interested in recruiting Marcus to come work for them in the near future.

As Emma's father escorted her toward the podium, she caught sight of the proud and dignified Edgar Zane standing in the front row. His tall, stunning wife, Olivia, was at his side. Both were wreathed in blinding smiles and happy tears over the miracle of having their son restored to him. As Emma glided closer, Olivia bent her head to kiss the dark-eyed, dark-haired grandson she'd hardly let out of her sight since their arrival into town. Jackson had the entire Zane side of the family wrapped around his tiny finger.

At the front of the church, Emma's closest and dearest friends waited. Clara was her matron of honor, and her other two bridesmaids stretched beyond her best friend in a stunning ripple of pink. Marcus's sister, Kiera brought to mind a dark goddess, and Axel's wife, Kristi, looked as exotic as a lotus blossom.

Marcus had chosen Axel Hammerstone as his

best man. Beyond Axel stood Dig MacLamore and Hunt Ryker. Four men who'd once served as Marines together and were now cemented for life by friendship.

Then Marcus stepped forward to claim Emma's attention, and all the other faces disappeared. Her heart pounded at how crazy handsome he looked in his white tuxedo. No amount of fancy silk and linen could hide such broach shoulders and ripped arms. He was her prince charming protector, her real-life hero, her partner for life.

"My bride," he declared huskily and bent to brush his lips against hers the moment her father handed her into his care. A sigh rose around them.

And so they renewed their vows in the presence of everyone who loved them. Afterward, Marcus glanced up and angled his head at someone in the back of the room.

Moments later, a chuckle worked its way across the sanctuary as Goliath pranced his way down the aisle.

"You didn't!" Emma's hand flew to her heart. Sure, it was unorthodox to have a dog in their wedding party, but Goliath was truly a part of their growing family. Sometimes serving as her work partner and lately as her nanny, he was so much more than a dog.

"Oh, but I did," her groom assured with a grin. "I

think everyone present agrees that he makes the perfect ring bearer."

So did she.

It took a few seconds of maneuvering and an excited bark or two from Goliath to release the black felt box from his collar. Marcus lifted the lid and there lay the diamond he'd promised her during their first wedding. It was a large, princess cut gem that made Emma feel like she'd stepped straight into the pages of a storybook.

While they gazed into each other's eyes, the minister gave his closing remarks and prayed a blessing over their lives. Then Marcus turned with her to face their gathering of friends and loved ones. But the ceremony wasn't quite over, as it turned out.

To their surprise, an honor guard of Marines had silently entered the sanctuary during their time of prayer. They were lined up on both sides of the aisle, stoically facing each other.

"Attention!" A general in a crisp Marine uniform weighed down with medals strode between their ranks. They snapped their heels to attention, and their hands went in unison to their temples to form a salute.

Oh, my...wow!

Marcus and Emma waited with their hands tightly clasped as he approached them.

"Ladies and gentlemen," the general boomed loudly enough to carry across the entire room.

The minister hurried around the podium to hand him a microphone.

The general nodded his thanks and continued speaking. "On behalf of the President of the United States, I am honored to conclude this ceremony with a presentation of the Congressional Medal of Honor to Sergeant Marcus Zane. For extraordinary valor on the battlefield in Kandahar, Afghanistan, to include the deliberate and willing risk of life and limb to save a comrade, to the subsequent and heroic sacrifice of the next fifteen months of his life as an undercover operative in order to save the lives of countless more fellow Marines, we are a truly grateful nation for your service." The general clicked his heels to attention and saluted Marcus.

Marcus saluted back. Then the general produced the hallowed medal, a gold star strung from a sky blue ribbon, and stretched on the toes of his shiny black low-quarters to drape it around Marcus's neck.

They shook hands. "Thank you, sir."

"The honor is all mine, sergeant." The general pivoted and marched back up the aisle in reverent silence. News cameras had flashed throughout the awards presentation and continued to flash as the general departed the sanctuary.

Then the room erupted into deafening cheers and clapping. Emma felt like weeping a whole ocean of happy tears and she witnessed her husband receiving the honors he so richly deserved.

He seemed uncertain what to do, opening his mouth as if to say something to her, then closing it without uttering a sound. That was the man she'd grown to love so much — strong but humble. He finally grinned and bent to kiss her cheek. "You could have at least warned me," he growled.

She gave him an innocent shrug to indicate she had nothing to do with the surprise award ceremony.

Instead of bubbles and confetti being tossed once their wedding party arrived outside, the Zane family had arranged for the honor guard of Marines to remain and fire a rifle volley.

Marcus dipped his head at the conclusion of the rifle fire to capture Emma's lips in a lingering kiss. "We earned this medal together," he muttered against her lips.

"I love you for saying that," she returned softly, "but trust me. You deserve every ounce of the honor they're giving you. I'm just so proud and so happy to be the wife of such an extraordinary man."

Red crept up his neck and darkened his face. "I couldn't have made it through the past year without you, sweetheart."

She smiled tenderly at him. "Well, you know what they say," she teased. "Behind every great man..."

"Nope. Not behind. I prefer to have you beside

me, Mrs. Zane." He bent to lift her in his arms. "Forever and always."

Then he carried her to the limousine idling at the curb, toward their joyous future together.

Like this book? Leave a review now!

Join Jo's List and never miss a new release or a great sale on her books.

Want to read about Officer Lincoln Hudson's search for happily-ever-after, now that his hopes in Emma's direction are, well, not going as planned? Poor Linc! He sure has great tastes in women, doesn't he? Keep turning the page for a sneak peek at his story, **THE GIRL NEXT DOOR RESCUE***! Then go read it all! Free in KU.*

Much love,
Jo

SNEAK PREVIEW: THE GIRL NEXT DOOR RESCUE

A K9 police officer in a country town, the sweetly stubborn blogger next door, and a dangerous storm that forces him to sweep her off her feet — literally!

Officer Lincoln Hudson has been recruited to run the K9 unit in Heart Lake, Texas. He feels like the luckiest guy on the planet to discover his neighbor is the rising DIY blogging sensation, The Perfect Fix. She's talented, entertaining, and hot! Unfortunately, she makes it clear she's a self-made, self-sufficient woman who doesn't need a man in her life.

When Katie Burke inherits a rambling old farmhouse, she jumps at the chance to trade in the fast-paced city for the peace of the country. It's also a way to put hundreds of miles between her and her ex, a man who pretended to love her while attempting to steal her business.

But Lincoln didn't get to where he is by giving up easily. He's determined to convince the woman he's falling for that a guy of his skill set is worth having around — especially during tornado season!

Grab your copy in eBook, paperback, or Kindle Unlimited on Amazon!
The Girl Next Door Rescue

Read them all!
The Plus One Rescue
The Secret Baby Rescue
The Bridesmaid Rescue
The Girl Next Door Rescue
The Secret Crush Rescue
The Bachelorette Rescue
The Rebound One Rescue
The Fake Bride Rescue
The Blind Date Rescue
The Maid by Mistake Rescue
The Unlucky Bride Rescue
The Temporary Family Rescue — *coming December, 2022!*

Much love,
Jo

NOTE FROM JO

Guess what? There's more going on in the lives of the hunky heroes you meet in my stories.

Because...*drum roll*...I have some Bonus Content for

everyone who signs up for my mailing list. From now on, there will be a special bonus content for each new book I write, just for my subscribers. Also, you'll hear about my next new book as soon as it's out (*plus you get a free book in the meantime*). Woohoo!

As always, thank you for reading and loving my books!

JOIN CUPPA JO READERS!

If you're on Facebook, please join my group, Cuppa Jo Readers. Don't miss out on the giveaways + all the sweet and swoony cowboys!

https://www.facebook.com/groups/
CuppaJoReaders

SNEAK PREVIEW: ACCIDENTAL HERO

After a bad breakup, former Army Ranger Matt Romero is on a new mission — to remain single.
What he's looking for can be boiled down to this:

- New job in a new town
- No relationship to complicate things

Rescuing a lovely cowgirl from a highway collision along the way is definitely not in the plan. Neither is the unexpected attraction it sparks, or her family's plea for him to stick around to help save their ranch from a whole string of trouble — an offer that all too quickly ignites into a second chance at love.

Matt has two choices. He can get back into his

truck and keep driving or stay long enough to find out if her half-paralyzed brother's claim is true — that sometimes the best things in life come when you're not even looking for them.

★ *BORN IN TEXAS is a sweet and inspirational romantic suspense series about small town, everyday heroes. Each book can be read as a standalone. Lots of heart, plenty of humor, and always a happily-ever-after!*

Accidental Hero
Available in eBook and paperback on Amazon + FREE in Kindle Unlimited!

Read them all!
A - Accidental Hero
B - Best Friend Hero
C - Celebrity Hero
D - Damaged Hero
E - Enemies to Hero
F - Forbidden Hero
G - Guardian Hero
H - Hunk and Hero
I - Instantly Her Hero

J - Jilted Hero
K - Kissable Hero

Much love,
Jo

SNEAK PREVIEW: HER BILLIONAIRE BOSS

Jacey Maddox didn't bother straightening her navy pencil skirt or smoothing her hand over the sleek lines of her creamy silk blouse. She already knew she looked her best. She knew her makeup was flawless, each dash of color accentuating her sun kissed skin and classical features. She knew this, because she'd spent way too many of her twenty-five years facing the paparazzi; and after her trust fund had run dry, posing for an occasional glossy centerfold — something she wasn't entirely proud of.

Unfortunately, not one drop of that experience lent her any confidence as she mounted the cold, marble stairs of Genesis & Sons. It towered more than twenty stories over the Alaskan Gulf waters, a stalwart high-rise of white and gray stone with tinted windows, a fortress that housed one of the world's most brilliant think tanks. For generations, the sons of Genesis had ridden the cutting edge of industrial design, developing the concepts behind some of the nation's most profitable inventions, products, and manufacturing processes.

It was the one place on earth she was least welcome.

Not just because of how many of her escapades had hit the presses during her rebel teen years. Not just because she'd possessed the audacity to marry their youngest son against their wishes. Not just because she had encouraged him to pursue his dreams instead of their hallowed corporate mission — a decision that had ultimately gotten him killed. No. The biggest reason Genesis & Sons hated her was because of her last name. The one piece of herself she'd refused to give up when she'd married Easton Calcagni.

Maddox.

The name might as well have been stamped across her forehead like the mark of the beast, as she moved into the crosshairs of their first security camera. It flashed an intermittent red warning light and gave a low electronic whirring sound as it swiveled to direct its lens on her.

Her palms grew damp and her breathing quickened as she stepped into the entry foyer of her family's greatest corporate rival.

Recessed mahogany panels lined the walls above a mosaic tiled floor, and an intricately carved booth anchored the center of the room. A woman with silver hair waving past her shoulders lowered her reading glasses to dangle from a pearlized chain. "May I help you?"

Jacey's heartbeat stuttered and resumed at a much faster pace. The woman was no ordinary receptionist. Her arresting blue gaze and porcelain features had graced the tabloids for years. She was Waverly, matriarch of the Calcagni family, grandmother to the three surviving Calcagni brothers. She was the one who'd voiced the greatest protests to Easton's elopement. She'd also wept in silence throughout his interment into the family mausoleum, while Jacey had stood at the edge of their gathering, dry-eyed and numb of soul behind a lacy veil.

The funeral had taken place exactly two months earlier.

"I have a one o'clock appointment with Mr. Luca Calcagni."

Waverly's gaze narrowed to twin icy points. "Not just any appointment, Ms. Maddox. You are here for an interview, I believe?"

Time to don her boxing gloves. "Yes." She could feel the veins pulsing through her temples now. She'd prepared for a rigorous cross-examination but had not expected it to begin in the entry foyer.

"Why are you really here?"

Five simple words, yet they carried the force of a full frontal attack. Beneath the myriad of accusations shooting from Waverly's eyes, she wanted to spin on her peep-toe stiletto pumps and run. Instead, she focused on regulating her breathing. It was a fair question. Her late husband's laughing face swam before her, both taunting and encouraging, as her mind ran over all the responses she'd rehearsed. None of them seemed adequate.

"I'm here because of Easton." It was the truth stripped of every excuse. She was here to atone for her debt to the family she'd wronged.

Pain lanced through the aging woman's gaze, twisting her fine-boned features with lines. Raw fury followed. "Do you want something from us, Ms. Maddox?" Condescension infused her drawling alto.

Not what you're thinking, that's for sure. I'm no gold-digger. "Yes. Very much. I want a job at Genesis." She could never restore Easton to his family, but she would offer herself in his place. She would spend the rest of her career serving their company in whatever capacity they would permit. It was the penance she'd chosen for herself.

The muscles around Waverly's mouth tightened a few degrees more. "Why not return to DRAW Corporation? To your own family?"

She refused to drop the elder woman's gaze as she absorbed each question, knowing they were shot like bullets to shatter her resolve, to remind her how unwelcome her presence was. She'd expected no other reception from the Calcagni dynasty; some would even argue she deserved this woman's scorn. However, she'd never been easily intimidated, a trait that was at times a strength and other times a curse. "With all due respect, Mrs. Calcagni, this *is* my family now."

Waverly's lips parted as if she would protest. Something akin to fear joined the choleric emotions churning across her countenance. She clamped her lips together, while her chest rose and fell several times. "You may take a seat now." She waved a heavily be-ringed hand to indicate the lounge area to her right. Lips pursed the skin around her mouth into papery creases, as she punched a few buttons on the call panel. "Ms. Maddox has arrived." Her frigid tone transformed each word into ice picks.

Jacey expelled the two painful clumps of air her lungs had been holding prisoner in a silent, drawn-out whoosh as she eased past the reception booth. She'd survived the first round of interrogations, a small triumph that yielded her no satisfaction. She knew the worst was yet to come. Waverly Calcagni was no more than a guard dog; Luca Calcagni was the one they sent into the boxing ring to finish off their opponents.

Luca apparently saw fit to allow her to marinate in her uneasiness past their appointment time. Not a surprise. He had the upper hand today and would do everything in his power to squash her with it. A full hour cranked away on the complicated maze of copper gears and chains on the wall. There was nothing ordinary about the interior of Genesis & Sons. Even their clocks were remarkable feats of architecture.

"Ms. Maddox? Mr. Calcagni is ready to see you."

She had to remind herself to breathe as she stood. At first she could see nothing but Luca's tall silhouette in the shadowed archway leading to the inner sanctum of Genesis & Sons. Then he took a step forward into a beam of sunlight and beckoned her to follow him. She stopped breathing again but somehow forced her feet to move in his direction.

He was everything she remembered and more from their few brief encounters. Much more. Up close, he seemed taller, broader, infinitely more intimidating, and so wickedly gorgeous it made her dizzy. That her parents had labeled him and his brothers as forbidden fruit made them all the more appealing to her during her teen years. It took her fascinated brain less than five seconds to recognize Luca had lost none of his allure.

The blue-black sheen of his hair, clipped short on the sides and longer on top, lent a deceptive innocence that didn't fool her one bit. Nor did the errant lock slipping to his forehead on one side. The expensive weave of his suit and complex twists of his tie far better illustrated his famed unpredictable temperament. His movements were controlled but fluid, bringing to her mind the restless prowl of a panther as she followed him down the hall and into an elevator. It shimmered with mirrored glass and recessed mahogany panels.

They rode in tense silence to the top floor.

Arrogance rolled off him from his crisply pressed white shirt, to his winking diamond and white gold cuff links, down to his designer leather shoes. In some ways, his arrogance was understandable. He guided the helm of one of the world's most profitable companies, after all. And his eyes! They were as beautiful and dangerous as the rest of him. Tawny with flecks of gold, they regarded her with open contempt as he ushered her from the elevator.

They entered a room surrounded by glass. One wall of windows overlooked the gulf waters. The other three framed varying angles of the Anchorage skyline. Gone was the old-world elegance of the first floor. This room was all Luca. A statement of power in chrome and glass. Sheer contemporary minimalism with no frills.

"Have a seat." It was an order, not an offer. A call to battle.

It was a battle she planned to win. She didn't want to consider the alternative — slinking back to her humble apartment in defeat.

He flicked one darkly tanned hand at the pair of Chinese Chippendale chairs resting before his expansive chrome desk. The chairs were stained black like the heart of their owner. No cushions.

They were not designed for comfort, only as a place to park guests whom the CEO did not intend to linger.

She planned to change his mind on that subject before her allotted hour was up. "Thank you." Without hesitation, she took the chair on the right, making no pretense of being in the driver's seat. This was his domain. Given the chance, she planned to mold herself into the indispensable right hand to whoever in the firm he was willing to assign her. On paper, she might not look like she had much to offer, but there was a whole pack of demons driving her. An asset he wouldn't hesitate to exploit once he recognized their unique value. Or so she hoped.

To her surprise, he didn't seat himself behind his executive throne. Instead, he positioned himself between her and his desk, hiking one hip on the edge and folding his arms. It was a deliberate invasion of her personal space with all six feet two of his darkly arresting half-Hispanic features and commanding presence.

Most women would have swooned.

Jacey wasn't most women. She refused to give him the satisfaction of either fidgeting or being the first to break the silence. Silence was a powerful weapon, something she'd learned at the knees of her parents. Prepared to use whatever it took to get what she'd come for, she allowed it to stretch well past the point of politeness.

Luca finally unfolded his arms and reached for the file sitting on the edge of his desk. "I read your application and resume. It didn't take long."

According to her mental tally, the first point belonged to her. She nodded to acknowledge his insult and await the next.

He dangled her file above the trash canister beside his desk and released it. It dropped and settled with a papery flutter.

"I fail to see how singing in nightclubs the past five years qualifies you for any position at Genesis & Sons."

The attack was so predictable she wanted to smile, but didn't dare. Too much was at stake. She'd made the mistake of taunting him with a smile once before. Nine years earlier. Hopefully, he'd long forgotten the ill-advised lark.

Or not. His golden gaze fixed itself with such intensity on her mouth that her insides quaked with uneasiness. Nine years later, he'd become harder and exponentially more ruthless. She'd be wise to remember it.

"Singing is one of art's most beautiful forms," she countered softly. "According to recent studies, scientists believe it releases endorphins and oxytocin while reducing cortisol." *There.* He wasn't the only one who'd been raised in a tank swimming with intellectual minds.

The tightening of his jaw was the only indication

her answer had caught him by surprise. Luca was a man of facts and numbers. Her answer couldn't have possibly displeased him, yet his upper lip curled. "If you came to sing for me, Ms. Maddox, I'm all ears."

The smile burgeoning inside her mouth vanished. Every note of music in her had died with her husband. That part of her life was over. "We both know I did not submit my employment application in the hopes of landing a singing audition." She started to rise, a calculated risk. "If you don't have any interest in conducting the interview you agreed to, I'll just excuse my—"

"Have a seat, Ms. Maddox." Her veiled suggestion of his inability to keep his word clearly stung.

She sat.

"Remind me what other qualifications you disclosed on your application. There were so few, they seem to have slipped my mind."

Nothing slipped his mind. She would bet all the money she no longer possessed on it. "A little forgetfulness is understandable, Mr. Calcagni. You're a very busy man."

Her dig hit home. This time the clench of his jaw was more perceptible.

Now that she had his full attention, she plunged on. "My strengths are in behind-the-scenes marketing as well as personal presentations. As you are well aware, I cut my teeth on DRAW Corporation's drafting tables. I'm proficient in an exhaustive list of software programs and a whiz at compiling slides, notes, memes, video clips, animated graphics, and most types of printed materials. My family just this morning offered to return me to my former position in marketing."

"Why would they do that?"

"They hoped to crown me Vice President of Communications in the next year or two. I believe their exact words were *it's my rightful place.*" As much as she tried to mask it, a hint of derision crept in her voice. There were plenty of employees on her family's staff who were far more qualified and deserving of the promotion.

His lynx eyes narrowed to slits. "You speak in the past tense, Ms. Maddox. After recalling what a flight risk you are, I presume your family withdrew their offer?"

It was a slap at her elopement with his brother. She'd figured he'd work his way around to it, eventually. "No." She deliberately bit her lower lip, testing him with another ploy that rarely failed in her dealings with men. "I turned them down."

His gaze locked on her mouth once more. Male interest flashed across his face and was gone. "Why?"

He was primed for the kill. She spread her hands and went for the money shot. "To throw myself at your complete mercy, Mr. Calcagni." The beauty of it was that the trembling in her voice wasn't faked; the request she was about to make was utterly genuine. "As your sister by marriage, I am not here to debate my qualifications or lack of them. I am begging you to give me a job. I need the income. I need to be busy. I'll take whatever position you are willing to offer so long as it allows me to come to work in this particular building." She whipped her face aside, no longer able to meet his gaze. "Here," she reiterated fiercely. "Where *he* doesn't feel as far away as he does outside these walls."

Because of the number of moments it took to compose herself, she missed his initial reaction to her words. When she tipped her face up to his once more, his expression was unreadable.

"Assuming everything you say is true, Ms. Maddox, and you're not simply up to another one of your games..." He paused, his tone indicating he thought she was guilty of the latter. "We do not currently have any job openings."

"That's not what your publicist claims, and it's certainly not what you have posted on your website." She dug through her memory to resurrect a segment of the Genesis creed. "Where innovation and vision collide. Where the world's most introspective minds are ever welcome—"

"Believe me, Ms. Maddox, I am familiar with our corporate creed. There is no need to repeat it. Especially since I have already made my decision concerning your employment."

Fear sliced through her. They were only five

minutes into her interview, and he was shutting her down. "Mr. Calcagni, I—"

He stopped her with an upraised hand. "You may start your two-week trial in the morning. Eight o'clock sharp."

He was actually offering her a job? Or, in this case, a ticket to the next round? According to her inner points tally, she hadn't yet accumulated enough to win. It didn't feel like a victory, either. She had either failed to read some of his cues, or he was better at hiding them than anyone else she'd ever encountered. She no longer had any idea where they stood with each other in their banter of words, who was winning and who was losing. It made her insides weaken to the consistency of jelly.

"Since we have no vacancies in the vice presidency category," he infused an ocean-sized dose of sarcasm into his words, "you'll be serving as my personal assistant. Like every other position on our payroll, it amounts to long hours, hard work, and no coddling. You're under no obligation to accept my offer, of course."

"I accept." She couldn't contain her smile this time. She didn't understand his game, but she'd achieved what she'd come for. Employment. No matter how humble the position. Sometimes it was best not to overthink things. "Thank you, Mr. Calcagni."

There was no answering warmth in him. "You won't be thanking me tomorrow."

"A risk I will gladly take." She rose to seal her commitment with a handshake and immediately realized her mistake.

Standing brought her nearly flush with her new boss. Close enough to catch a whiff of his aftershave — a woodsy musk with a hint of cobra slithering her way. Every organ in her body suffered a tremor beneath the full blast of his scrutiny.

When his long fingers closed over hers, her insides radiated with the same intrinsic awareness of him she'd experienced nine years ago — the day they first met.

It was a complication she hadn't counted on.

I hope you enjoyed this excerpt from
Her Billionaire Boss
*Available in eBook and paperback on Amazon +
FREE in Kindle Unlimited!*

Much love,
Jo

ALSO BY JO GRAFFORD

For the most up-to-date printable list of my books:

Click here

or go to:

https://www.JoGrafford.com/books

For the most up-to-date printable list of books by Jo Grafford, writing as Jovie Grace (*sweet historical romance*):

Click here

or go to:

https://www.jografford.com/joviegracebooks

ABOUT JO

Jo is an Amazon bestselling author of sweet and inspirational romance stories about faith, hope, love and family drama with a few Texas-sized detours into comedy. She also writes sweet and inspirational historical romance as Jovie Grace.

1.) Follow on Amazon!
amazon.com/author/jografford

2.) Join Cuppa Jo Readers!
https://www.facebook.com/groups/
CuppaJoReaders

3.) Follow on Bookbub!

https://www.bookbub.com/authors/jo-grafford

4.) Follow on Instagram!
https://www.instagram.com/jografford/

5.) Follow on YouTube
https://www.youtube.com/channel/
UC3R1at97Qso6BXiBIxCjQ5w

amazon.com/authors/jo-grafford

bookbub.com/authors/jo-grafford

facebook.com/jografford

instagram.com/jografford

pinterest.com/jografford